THE BILLIONAIRE OP

THE SUTTON BILLIONAIRES SERIES, BOOK 3

LORI RYAN

OTHER BOOKS BY LORI RYAN

The Sutton Billionaires Series:

The Billionaire Deal

Reuniting with the Billionaire

The Billionaire Op

The Billionaire's Rock Star

The Billionaire's Navy SEAL

Falling for the Billionaire's Daughter (May 2020)

The Sutton Capital Intrigue Series:

Cutthroat

Cut and Run

Cut to the Chase

The Sutton Capital on the Line Series:

Pure Vengeance

Latent Danger

The Triple Play Curse Novellas:

Game Changer

Game Maker

Game Clincher

The Heroes of Evers, TX Series:

Love and Protect

Promise and Protect

Honor and Protect (An Evers, TX Novella)

Serve and Protect

Desire and Protect

Cherish and Protect

Treasure and Protect

The Dark Falls, CO Series:

Dark Falls

Dark Burning

Dark Prison

Coming Soon – The Halo Security Series:

Dulce's Defender

Hannah's Hero

Shay's Shelter

Callie's Cover

Grace's Guardian

Sophie's Sentry

Sienna's Sentinal

For the most current list of Lori's books, visit her website: loriryanromance.com.

ACKNOWLEDGMENTS

I'd like to thank my incredibly supportive husband and my kids for putting up with the madness of deadlines and rewrites. Thank you to Sue and Cathy for all of the brainstorming and reading drafts. Thank you to Patricia Thomas for editing, copy-editing, and working with such tight deadlines and turn-arounds. Thank you to Emme Adams of Novel Ideas Editing for developmental contributions. And, thank you to Patricia Parent for being my final set of eyes.

AUTHOR'S NOTE

If you love this book and want to read two novellas in the series for free, sign up for my newsletter here and I'll send them to you: loriryanromance.com/thebakernovellas

CHAPTER 1

*C*had Thompson woke to searing pain in his chest as he gulped air, desperate to fill his battered lungs. He squeezed his eyes shut and battled to clear the fog from his head and slow his heart rate.

This was wrong. It was all wrong. He caught hold of the sounds around him and forced himself to listen to them, knowing they would ground him: the sound of traffic on the street below his window and the hum of his air conditioner kicking on as it reached the designated temperature. Chad shook his head and forced his eyes open.

He was in his bedroom in New Haven, Connecticut, in his bed with the navy-blue sheets and mahogany headboard. Above him was the familiar crack on the ceiling that he always meant to fix but never remembered to unless he was in bed staring up at it. His flat-screen television, mounted on the wall, ran static. His laptop lay on the bed next to him where he'd abandoned it for sleep the night before.

Despite the familiar surroundings, it took Chad a minute to realize there was no medic kneeling beside him, pushing a too-long needle into his lung. There was no metallic scent of blood or charred flesh choking him and making him nauseated.

No ringing in his ears. The other three men in his detail did not lay still and silent beside him, their eyes lifeless and unseeing, their bodies forever broken and destroyed.

The dream didn't come often anymore, but it always took him a few minutes to recover when it did. As Chad took deep, calming breaths he realized his phone was ringing. He slapped at the nightstand with one hand until he found the phone then slid his thumb across the screen to answer the call.

"Yeah?" His voice was thick with sleep.

"Chad?"

He bolted upright in his bed, the remnants of the dream no longer clutching at him. His gut twisted when Jennie's voice came through the phone with the ring of false confidence. Something wasn't right.

"You okay, Jennie?"

Jennie Evans didn't normally call him outside of working hours at Sutton Capital. They had a weird relationship. Chad was Jennie's boss. She was flippant, irreverent, and completely brash in all her dealings with him. And, he loved it.

Outside of work, things were equally unorthodox between them. They spent a lot of time together because Jennie was best friends with Kelly, the woman who married Chad's cousin last year. Jack and Chad were more like brothers than cousins. So Chad saw Jennie almost anytime he hung out with Jack and Kelly, which was just about every weekend.

But, Chad and Jennie weren't the type of friends that called each other or sought one another out outside of the group. It was more that they ended up at the same functions because of their mutual relationships.

So when she called on his cell phone first thing on a Sunday morning, he noticed.

It was also the use of his name that got his attention. Quickly.

Jennie didn't use a nickname like 'Boss Man,' 'Big Man,' or 'the Hulk' like she usually did. No, this morning she called him

Chad, rather than any number of other nicknames designed to taunt him about his large stature.

"Um. I'm a little...stuck," Jennie said on the other end of the phone. He could hear her hesitancy through the line.

"Define 'stuck,' Jennie." As he talked, he threw back the covers and swung his legs over the edge of the bed.

"I'm out at Edgerton Park and I don't have any shoes to jog home. Can you come get me? Jack and Kelly are touring the Labor and Delivery Unit at the hospital this morning so I can't call them and I can't get hold of Jill, either" Jennie said.

Jill was married to Chad's friend Andrew who also worked at Sutton Capital.

"How did you get out to Edgerton Park without shoes or a car?" Chad asked as he shoved his feet into sneakers.

As he spoke, the implications of what he'd just said sank into his brain. Jennie was alone in a park without shoes or a way to get home. Fear for her rippled up his spine, but he tamped it down and focused.

He moved a lot faster, as his mind began to play through scenarios. Was she with a guy and he ditched her? Was she out drunk last night and never made it home? Maybe she found herself in the park, with no shoes and no idea how she got there?

Just the thought of Jennie out with a guy started a slow burn in his gut, not that he had any right to be upset about that. Chad couldn't date her since he was her boss, but if a man treated her wrong or hurt her in any way. . . he sure as hell wouldn't tolerate that.

I'll kill whatever asshole did this to her.

"Can I tell you when you get here? I've been here for a while now. I'm getting a little hungry. And my feet hurt. I had to run in bare feet. I could really use a ride."

Run? She'd been running...

Chad's fists turned into hard knots of anger as he thought

about someone leaving Jennie where she could have been hurt or... Another thought sent cold spiraling through him.

God, what if they didn't just ditch her at the park? What if...? His heart pounded in his chest and he broke out in a sweat.

Now Chad used the eerily calm tone of voice from his days in the military. It came out when he was pissed as hell and ready to tear someone to pieces, but also when he needed to keep himself calm and collected enough to deal with the situation.

"Jennie, did someone hurt you?"

"I'm okay, Chad. No one hurt me," she answered, sending a wave of relief over him that left him weak—much weaker than he'd acknowledge. He grabbed his wallet and keys.

"On my way."

"Thanks, Chad. I'm over by the greenhouses. I'll wait by that entrance," Jennie said.

The park was well known for the large row of greenhouses that boasted an impressive array of native plants. The local gardening club held a native plant sale twice a year. There was an entrance cut into the stone wall that surrounded the park, near those greenhouses. Chad knew it well. It was the entrance he used whenever he jogged through the park.

"Got it," Chad said as he ended the call and grabbed a T-shirt. He pulled the shirt on as he rode the elevator to the garage and jogged to his truck.

What the hell, Jennie?

He didn't know what story she'd have when he got there, but this sounded like a bit much, even for Jennie.

Explaining this to Chad wouldn't be fun. How do you explain that you had to run from guard dogs with half your clothes missing because they snuck up on you when you were skinny dipping in some guy's pool?

When Jennie had been running from the dogs, she was laughing. When she'd climbed the fence and run through a stranger's backyard to get away, it had still been kind of funny. When she couldn't find anyone other than Chad to come out and get her, she'd stopped laughing.

Kelly or Jill would have laughed with her. Even Jack or Andrew probably would have laughed a little. Chad? Not so much. He wouldn't be amused and he wouldn't hesitate to lecture her. And lecture her. And lecture her.

She spotted Chad's black F350 as he turned onto Cliff Street. She had to force herself to stand still and keep her head raised. If she fidgeted, he'd see it as a sign of weakness and that would only make things worse.

Jennie twisted her long hair, squeezing the excess water from it. What a sight she must be. Her hair was wet, she was missing her shoes and her bra, and her T-shirt was torn and dirty. And if he noticed her limping, he'd probably drag her off to the hospital. Chad was nothing, if not overprotective.

And...there's the scowl.

Jennie wished, for once, he wouldn't look so damned sexy. She didn't know how it was possible for someone to look so good and still have such an angry expression, but he looked gorgeous no matter what he was doing.

Maybe it was the dangerous edge he presented. Anyone who knew Chad knew he was a sweet teddy bear on the inside, but on the outside he looked like he could do some serious damage.

On a sigh, Jennie opened the door and climbed up into the large cab of Chad's truck. She knew he'd picked his truck to fit himself comfortably. Unfortunately, it dwarfed everyone else, making it a project for Jennie to get in and out. She shimmied up and plopped into the passenger seat.

Settling herself, Jennie buckled her seatbelt and raised her face to Chad's. She tilted her head to the side and took in Chad's brooding gaze. A shiver of awareness went through her body as she felt his damn eyes on her.

Down, girl.

As usual, her body refused to listen to her when it came to Chad. It ran amuck, responding to every look, every whisper, and every grumble that came from those sexy lips in that low, controlled tone of his. Oh, what she wouldn't do to see him lose that control.

No! I don't want that. It's only my stupid, traitorous body that wants that.

"Hey, Tiny," she said. "I'd offer to buy you breakfast, but with no shoes, I'm afraid we couldn't get in anywhere respectable."

She put on her best cheeky grin and hoped he would ignore the embarrassing state of her clothing. Or, lack thereof.

Chad was apparently of a different mind and let his eyes roam from her face, down her body and back up again. Of course, his gaze felt like hands grazing her body and that lit her up from the inside. Somehow, she knew his hands would feel even more amazing on her. Caressing, roaming freely, they would set her ablaze.

Stupid body.

He kept his eyes on hers as he reached over and turned off the ignition with a short, economic movement. Then, he sat. Waited.

Great. He's in interrogation mode.

She rolled her eyes. "Really?"

"Really." His was a statement not a question and she realized that, yes, he really was going to wait until she spilled the story. She sighed heavily, hoping he would give up.

Damn. The man's got military training and I've got diddly.

"You realize I'm an adult, right? I don't actually need to tell you what I was doing. You get that, right?"

Jennie could have sworn she saw the side of his mouth twitch and wondered for a split second if he was tempted to smile. *No. Not Chad.*

"I can always let you out and just go home, Jennie. I'm an adult. I don't actually need to drive you home. You get that, right?" he mimicked her words.

She narrowed her eyes at him. "You wouldn't..."

Chad shrugged as if he really might consider leaving Jennie there. They both knew he wouldn't.

"I was jogging. All right? I jog out here every morning." She laid her hands in her lap as if that answered everything and looked back at Chad with what she hoped was her best wide-eyed and innocent gaze. Oh, why did her belly feel like a hundred can-can girls were practicing in there with their puffy can-can skirts whipping around?

One tanned, muscled arm rested on the steering wheel of the truck, the other lay between him and Jennie on the seat. She tried not to notice the muscles rippling under his T-shirt or how good he smelled.

He'd clearly been sleeping when she called him. He probably just rolled out of bed, threw on sweats – and he somehow managed to look like walking sex and smell spicy and woodsy... She licked her lips.

Chad, who'd been studying her face, looked pointedly down at her bare feet, then flicked his eyes back up to hers and waited. That earned him another eye roll and a huff of frustration.

"Fine. I jog out here every morning. There's a house on Prospect Court that has a pool. The guy is never home. He travels a lot," Jennie explained in clipped tones.

"You know this, how?" Chad asked, but made no move to start the truck.

She could see the small tick in his jaw that struck when she was really needling him. Sometimes, she could turn the tick into a smile, if she worked hard at it. She wondered if she'd be able to do that now, but wasn't sure she could risk it. If she pushed too hard at the wrong time, things might go in the other direction and she'd be in for a lecture.

Not that a lecture from him was all that bad. She could zone out and stare at the way his shirt stretched across the hard planes of his chest or the evidence of a six pack she could see just below it. But, she would like to shower sooner rather than later. She was starting to feel really grimy.

"My friend dated him for a while," Jennie shrugged. "Can we go now?"

Chad raised an eyebrow but remained silent.

A frustrated sigh burst past Jennie's lips, as she shook her head at him. "Fine, I jog here, let myself in through the back gate, go for a swim, and then jog home. It's my morning routine. I always peek to see if his car's in the garage. If it is, I skip my swim. He must have realized someone's been in his yard. I had just gotten in the pool when I heard barking. The next thing I know, there are two big dogs blasting out of a doggy door and heading my way. They were on the side of the yard with the gate, so I had to go over the back of the fence instead and cut through the neighbor's yard. I grabbed what I could and ran. My shoes weren't in the pile of stuff I grabbed."

Jennie drew her spine up straight and laced her fingers together in her lap. It wasn't easy to look dignified in the state she was in, but she could damn well try.

Chad stared at Jennie for a few more long seconds. The tick in his jaw continued as his eyes burned into her with an intensity that almost stole her breath. She raised her chin and resisted the very strong urge to squirm.

"Neither was your bra, apparently," he said dryly as he reached for the keys and started the truck. He shoved the gear into place and pulled away from the curb as Jennie laughed, wrapping her arms firmly in place over her chest.

CHAPTER 2

*O*ver lunch at their favorite café, Jennie told her best friends, Kelly and Jill, about her narrow escape that morning. She recounted the story of the dogs, the fence, losing her shoes and her long ride home with Chad lecturing her about dog bites and what could have happened if she'd been caught.

Kelly and Jill wiped tears from their eyes. The waitress probably thought they were all crazy. They'd been laughing for five minutes straight, with Jennie barely able to squeak out the details of her morning between impressions of Chad scowling.

Kelly and Jill were Jennie's two closest friends, aside from a few high school friends back home that she didn't see very often.

"I'll bet you had him grinding his teeth the whole ride." Kelly laughed, but then groaned and held her pregnant belly. "You have to stop making me laugh. The baby kicks more when I laugh and she's tap dancing on vital organs right now."

Jennie grinned as she sipped her iced tea. "Sorry, Kels. I'll try to be more serious until you deliver. What's that, five more weeks?"

Her friend grimaced. "Don't remind me."

"I think Chad thought it was funny, though. He likes to act all tough, but he's just a big teddy bear." Jennie nodded, as though trying to convince the others with body language when she knew her argument was falling flat.

Jill shook her head. "Quit poking the damn bear, Jennie. It's not safe."

Jennie grinned. "I just hope he doesn't show up at my house tomorrow morning to escort me on my morning run."

"He wouldn't do that!" Jill said, then looked at Kelly for confirmation.

"Oh, he might. I told him I was thinking of bringing dog treats tomorrow. I'll bet I can make friends with those dogs and get my morning swim back," Jennie said.

That started the laughter again and left poor Kelly holding her stomach.

The three of them were like Charlie's Angels in a way, each with a completely different look. Kelly was the brunette, with a curvy body even when she wasn't pregnant, and a smile that was contagious.

Jill was the blonde in the group. She had gorgeous hazel eyes that Jennie was secretly a bit envious of and she was more willowy than Jennie and Kelly.

Jennie was a few inches shorter than her two friends, with strawberry-blond hair that hung in wild curls. She'd given up trying to tame it a long time ago. She'd always thought her brown eyes were plain looking, but Kelly said they were rich and deep so Jennie had decided to believe her.

Kelly was married to Jack Sutton, the Chief Executive Officer at Sutton Capital, where Jennie worked. Jill had just married Andrew Weston. Andrew was Jack's best friend and the Chief Financial Officer at Sutton. They were a tight-knit group of friends who worked closely together and saw one another almost every weekend without fail.

Jennie knew that would change now that Jack and Kelly were having a baby and Jill and Andrew had just married. It hurt to think her life might be changing once again as her friends moved on to a life that couldn't include her in the same way it always had.

Sure, she'd no doubt be Auntie Jen to all their children, but it wouldn't be the same as having her own family and having kids alongside her best friends. Jill broke through Jennie's thoughts.

"Hey, I keep forgetting to ask you. Where did you go on your last assignment? Anywhere fun and exciting?" Jill asked. She and Andrew had taken care of Jennie's dog, Zeke, a few weeks ago when Jennie was traveling for Sutton.

She made a face. "To a biotech company in Wisconsin. The people were really nice but there wasn't a whole lot to do. They were in the middle of nowhere."

Jennie was sure she had one of the most unusual jobs on the planet. Sutton Capital was a venture capital firm that invested in startup companies and in companies looking to expand or to develop new technologies.

Although Jennie had started out as a temporary assistant, she now worked in the security and investigations division. She'd always thought Jack was crazy for promoting her, but Jack didn't operate like a conventional CEO, and Jennie wasn't about to question his decision.

She loved it more than she'd ever loved any job. She had floated from one temporary job to another after college, finding most of them dull and unchallenging. Her work at Sutton Capital was anything but dull. It just fit her, somehow.

When Jennie wasn't out of the office on assignment, she worked as a floating assistant helping anyone around the company that needed her. When on assignment, she was sent into a company that was trying to get funding from Sutton or that Sutton was considering purchasing. Jennie would typically go in with someone from finance or occasionally someone from legal who was doing due diligence. She'd serve as their assistant, but in reality, she had a dual purpose.

She was tasked with quickly befriending people and getting

them to talk to her. She usually acted like an airhead when she was on assignment, babbling on and on and laughing just a little too much at things. It reminded her of her days in drama club in high school. She'd played Audrey her senior year in Little Shop of Horrors and she always drew from the ditsy portrayal when she went on a new assignment.

When she took on that persona, people just opened right up to her. Then, it was just a matter of keeping her ears open for any information that might help Jack make decisions about the potential investment. Sometimes support staff she befriended would tell her juicy bits of gossip that might contain nuggets of information. Other times, executives in the company talked freely in front of her, assuming she was either too dumb to understand what they were talking about or too flighty to pay attention.

Jennie would never forget the time the two principals in a company sat in front of her and talked about the fact they had doctored the numbers they gave Jack – as if she weren't even in the room. She sat collating papers at the conference table, keeping her head down while they met over lunch and spilled the whole story.

She would have been offended at the way the two men dismissed her so completely, if she hadn't known how valuable the information she gathered would be. That information ended up saving Jack and his investors a lot of money.

"Never mind what the night life was like in Wisconsin, did you find out anything juicy?" Kelly asked. Jill and Kelly loved hearing what Jennie discovered during her assignments.

"No. Well, other than the fact two of the researchers like to play doctor after hours in the lab together." Jennie shivered and laughed. "It wasn't something I ever need to see again."

Kelly and Jill laughed.

"It couldn't have been that bad!" Jill said.

"Oh, but it was. They were not attractive people, to say the least, and I got a real eyeful! I had to go back to my hotel room and scrub my eyes with a pumice stone."

The three women laughed as the waitress brought their meals and they dug into chips and sandwiches.

"I told Chad I want combat pay for that assignment, but he told me to take it up with Jack, so you need to back me on it, Kels."

As they finished up their lunches, Jennie looked at her two best friends and silently hoped they'd be able to stay as close as they were today despite the changes that were coming. Her friends were moving toward a life that she'd already lost. Jennie's happily-ever-after had ended years before, and there wasn't any way she could get it back.

CHAPTER 3

*C*had suppressed a grin as he watched Jennie. At the moment, they were in the pool at Kelly and Jack's house, where everyone had gathered for one last party before the baby arrived. Chad stood on one side of a pool volleyball net and Jennie stood on the other. Somewhere along the way, he'd forgotten what Jennie was arguing about, but he didn't care.

It might be chauvinistic, but he loved seeing her fiery eyes sparkle as she fisted small hands on her hips and lit into him. She barely reached his chest, but she should get points for trying. Jennie tossed her head, flinging her strawberry-blond curls out behind her and kept right on going.

He loved this side of her. She was bold and brash and confident. She was feisty and fun loving and nothing seemed to frighten her. Not many women Jennie's size – a mere 5'4" and 115 pounds if he was guessing right – would try the irreverent things she did with Chad.

At 6'4" and about 265 pounds of pure muscle, there weren't many people who treated Chad the way Jennie did. She taunted and teased him at every turn, as if she was two or three feet taller.

Chad knew why she did it. They both felt the wild attraction that sizzled between them and they both worked hard to control it. With so many mutual friends, coupled with the fact that they worked together all day during the week, they couldn't avoid seeing one another.

So Jennie seemed to deal with the attraction by throwing her saucy, cheeky attitude at him all the time. It was almost as if she tried to keep their interactions superficial, never going deeper than the surface. If she was busy yelling at him or taunting him, there wasn't room for anything else.

Chad dealt with the attraction by staying in complete and utter control at all times around her. He didn't allow himself to dwell on the curve of her tiny waist or the swell of her breasts in the bikini she wore as she fought with him now. He focused on her eyes, ignoring her body.

Then, he'd spend about five minutes telling himself that her eyes were nothing special. He'd tell himself her eyes weren't warm and rich like melted caramel. That her eyes didn't have a mysterious quality to them as if she held a world of secrets waiting for him to explore.

Shit. So much for control.

Chad wondered if Jennie would keep up her tirade if she knew just how sexy she was when she was angry. Or if she'd keep up the nicknames if she knew how much he liked to see what she'd call him next. Would it be 'Tank' today or 'Little Bit?' Or maybe "Mini Man."

Jennie cupped her hand and splashed water across the net at Chad, pulling him from his thoughts.

Yeah, so much for maintaining control.

"Are you even listening to me, Chad?"

Nope. Chad's grin broke through as he shook his head, willing it to clear. "Sorry, Jen. I tuned out five minutes ago."

He knew that would really get her going and he'd get to watch her fume for a while longer. He could watch Jennie Evans storm at him forever and not get tired of it.

~

As the day wound down, Jennie wandered away from the pool and sat in one of the teak chairs that faced the back lawn of Jack and Kelly's house on Long Island Sound in Connecticut. The sprawling house had become one of the main gathering places for their group in the summer. With a yard that sloped down to a small private beach and a pool with outdoor kitchen, it was perfect for barbeques and parties.

A welcome cool breeze brushed gently over Jennie's bare arms. She curled her feet under her on the chaise lounge and listened to the noises of the party, letting them engulf her. The sounds of her friends laughing and talking soothed her.

Her black lab, Zeke, had given up playing with Zoe, the mixed breed puppy Jack and Kelly had rescued from the shelter, and Jill's labradoodle, Rev. Zeke now lay, snoring loudly, but she was sure he'd open his eyes in a heartbeat if anyone dropped even a bite of food nearby. The six-year-old dog gave new meaning to the term 'chowhound.'

Jennie's eyes landed on Jill and Andrew walking hand in hand toward the beach. She smiled as she watched Jill lean into Andrew, who said something that made Jill laugh. After heartache neither one of them deserved, they had finally found each other. They'd been married in the spring and had just moved into a new home in New Haven. Jennie knew they were both eager to have children and Jill had mentioned that they wanted to start trying for a baby right away. She was happy for the new couple.

Today's party was Kelly and Jack's last chance to host a get together before their first baby came. Kelly was due in just three weeks, and even though she looked exhausted as she sat with Jack's arms around her, she looked happier than Jennie had ever seen her. And that made Jennie happy.

Roark Walker, Jack's lawyer and longtime family friend, was

trying to help Jack's housekeeper, Mrs. Poole, carry leftovers into the house. She was shooing him away with a scowl. The two were always fussing at one another for some reason, but even that made Jennie smile. It was comfortable and familiar. Like family, in a way.

Her eyes found Chad, who stood on the opposite side of the pool, beer in hand as he talked to friends. She felt the familiar quickening of her breath that always happened when she looked at him. Her eyes roamed over his strong chest and muscled arms, the broad shoulders of his imposing frame.

His dark looks—even with the smattering of scars that etched his skin from his time serving in the military overseas— rivaled those of the biggest and brightest stars of Hollywood. In spite of that, there wasn't an arrogant bone in Chad's body. This, of course, made him all the more attractive.

The man was stunningly handsome, unquestionably kind and gentle, and he sent the bones in Jennie's body into a puddle on the floor when he glanced her way.

She didn't want to be attracted to him. But, she found she couldn't ignore his effect on her no matter how she tried. And that, unfortunately, tore at her heart. Jennie wished with all her being that Chad Thompson didn't have such a powerful effect on her.

When she had first met Chad, she tried to find his faults. If she could get herself to see him as an arrogant jerk, she might be able to ignore the physical attraction she felt for him. It would certainly make it easier to resist him, anyway.

Since Chad was born into the Sutton family, he could have sat back and reaped the benefits of the family business without actually doing any work. He only worked until three o'clock many days, making Jennie assume he was living off of trust fund money and not really contributing at all. That made it easier to resist the outward allure for a little while.

Sadly, her first impressions didn't last and Jennie soon had to admit that Chad was just as attractive a person on the inside as he was on the outside. It turned out he left work early to volunteer at a nearby veteran's hospital.

And the more Jennie got to know Chad, the more apparent it became that he was anything but a selfish, spoiled trust fund brat. That certainly didn't make it easier for her to resist him. But, she knew in her heart, she didn't want a relationship with him or anyone else. She didn't want the chemistry between them to exist.

"Hey, sweetie," Kelly said as she lowered herself into the chair next to Jennie. She wasn't moving very gracefully. "I swear, this baby has an elbow in my lung right now. She somehow gets up under my ribs and digs in and won't let go."

Jennie grinned at Kelly. "I can't wait for that baby to get here."

Kelly snorted. "You and me both."

Jennie nodded toward the other side of the pool where her coworker and friend, Samantha Page was talking to Kelly's sister, Jesse. The two were opposites, physically. Samantha was tall with dark hair that hung down her back. Jesse was petite with honey blonde hair.

"I'm glad to see Sam," Jennie said. "She looks like she's doing a lot better."

Samantha might work at Sutton Capital, but she was often included in lists of the country's top hackers, sometimes even topping the list. She recently took time off to help the FBI track a group of women who had been sold into sexual slavery. It hit her hard and she'd had a rough time dealing with the emotional toll of the work. They were all worried about her.

Kelly nodded. "She is. She's back at work and she's been working on her game again."

Jennie grinned. "She let me try a beta version of the game. It freaking rocks."

Samantha had been working on a multiplayer online fantasy game and they were all waiting for her to release it when it was ready.

"No fair!" Kelly said. She pouted in Samantha's direction even though the other woman couldn't hear her.

Jennie laughed at Kelly and raised her hands in the air. "Hey, don't blame me." She smirked. "Besides, she said she's going to let you try it this weekend."

Kelly scowled. "Hmmm, I guess that's okay." Kelly grinned then. "Did she tell you the name she's picked out?"

Now it was Jennie's turn to pout. "No! What do you know, woman?"

Kelly laughed and made a zipping gesture over her lips. "I'm sworn to secrecy."

"Then why did you ask me?"

Kelly lifted a shoulder in a shrug as she grinned. "Because if you knew then we could talk about it." She looked at Jennie then, growing serious. "How're you holding up?"

Jennie tilted her head back and forth. "I'm good. Hangin' in."

Jennie sipped the last bit of lemonade from her glass before setting it on the table next to her. "Oh, Jeez, Zeke. Cut that out!" Jennie shooed Zeke down off the table where he'd been busy stealing the remnants of a hotdog off someone's plate. She hadn't even seen him get up.

Kelly laughed as the dog-slash-garbage-disposal swallowed down the hotdog in one bite, not looking the least bit chagrined at being caught stealing food. But when she looked back to Jennie, Jennie could see the concern in Kelly's expression.

"I forget sometimes, you know. Until days like this and then it hits me that this probably hurts like hell for you." Kelly reached out and held Jennie's hand, squeezing. Her voice was lowered now, maintaining the private nature of the topic she'd just broached.

Jennie appreciated Kelly's commitment to keeping her secrets. She shrugged and plastered her standard smile on her face. This wasn't a conversation she wanted to have. "It is what it is. I can't change it so why dwell?"

She could tell her friend didn't buy her act and if Kelly was thinking Jennie's smile was just for show, she was right. Some days, it was all an act.

But, for the most part, she'd found happiness with her friends and her life at Sutton Capital. They were really good friends she treasured. And, she loved her work. After feeling like she was floating around untethered, with no real goals for years, she finally had a job she loved.

Good friends and a good job. That was all Jennie could hope for.

Kelly reached over and put her hand on her friend's arm. "I'm sorry, honey. I wish things were different. It isn't fair."

Jennie just nodded and swallowed. Hard. Her chest tightened and she willed away the lump caught in her throat and the tears that threatened to fall. Four years later and she still had a hard time talking about it.

She and her husband, Kyle, had been more than just high school sweethearts. They grew up next door to each other, were best friends through junior high, dated in high school, and managed to keep their relationship strong through four years of college.

The year they graduated from college, they married. By the following year, Kyle was gone – he'd lost his fight with cancer a few short months after his diagnosis and just two days after their first anniversary.

Jennie still couldn't stomach vanilla cupcakes – the memory of the vanilla cupcake her mother-in-law brought her and Kyle in the hospital for their anniversary was too strong and painful.

Jennie and Kelly had only been friends for two years, and it had been awhile before Jennie told Kelly about her husband. The rest of the group had no idea she had ever been married.

"I'm okay. Honestly, it's harder sometimes with my friends who knew Kyle and me. They never forget. Kyle was like a part of my identity with them. With you, I get to forget. Or, at least pretend for a while. But, I'm good. I'm happy for you guys. For all of you."

She looked out over the lawn at Andrew and Jill, and at Jesse and Zach, then glanced to where Jack watched Kelly as only a man waiting for the arrival of his first child does. His look seemed to encompass so many emotions: everything from sheer joy to excitement to fear of the unknown.

Neither said anything else. There wasn't really anything left to say. The two friends sat quietly as Kelly's kick-off-to-motherhood party wound down.

Chad watched his mother as she walked around the pool to approach him. Until recently, he and his mother had a tumultuous relationship. For several years she'd been so angry over his father leaving her, she'd lashed out at all of the people around her.

Oddly enough, Kelly's marriage to Jack had helped her get over that and Chad was glad to have his mom back to her old self —overbearing and pushy, but now full of love instead of hate and spite.

Chad looked down as he scrubbed at the grill in Jack's outdoor kitchen with a wire brush. The party had dwindled to close friends and family, and the cleanup had begun.

Mabry Thompson sidled up to her son and sipped her wine as she looked out over the few remaining family members and friends. She ran a hand up and down his back as if he were still five years old and she could soothe him that way.

"Is it hard to watch Jack and Andrew starting their own families?"

Chad knew his mother left off the part of the question she

really wanted to ask. She wanted to ask if it bothered him to be left behind as his best friend and cousin moved forward.

He shrugged a shoulder at her. "It's not like they're leaving me, Mom. We still work together, hang out together, see each other everyday."

Chad cringed as he felt his eyes travel to Jennie before he could school himself.

He'd been out of the military too long. His guard was slipping. *Damn. I should know better.*

Mabry didn't miss the glance and she didn't bother to pull punches with her son. "Do you ever wonder if you do it on purpose, Chad?"

Now his gaze shot to his mother and his hand stilled for a minute as he studied her. "Do what on purpose?"

"Choose women you can't have. It's safer that way. Lord knows, I get that. But, you won't ever be happy if you continue to make the choices you do. Do you wonder sometimes if you're sabotaging yourself on purpose? If you've made sure you haven't found love and happiness and a family because if you do that, you'll really have to deal with the guilt of coming home safe? Of being here when others aren't?"

Chad stopped cleaning the grill and looked down at his mother. How this woman who was five feet, two inches had given birth to large man like him remained a mystery. "Clearly you do. What makes you think I would sabotage my own happiness, Mom?"

She looked at her son for a long time. Long enough to irritate the tar out of him, but he didn't let her see that. He met her stare and waited, not speaking. Not squirming under her gaze.

Finally his mother spoke. "I know you think you don't have the baggage that a lot of your friends came back with, but sometimes I wonder if that's really true."

Chad considered himself lucky. Damn lucky. He'd come home from three tours of duty with a few scars and, yes, with horrifying memories and dreams that sometimes haunted him. But, he hadn't been seriously injured.

He didn't suffer from post-traumatic stress, where the dreams followed you into the daylight, making you edgy and anxious and irritable. He was able to function normally most of the time. And, most of all, he had his life. He had lived. That was more than a lot of the men he served with had.

When he first came home, he tried to isolate himself, unable to face being back in a world that functioned so differently from the one he'd known overseas.

But, Jack and Andrew hadn't let him hide himself away. They were there day after day, pulling him back into the world. He knew he wouldn't have found his way back without their support.

So Chad had seen a counselor and he now worked with other veterans, helping them adjust to life at home. It was with this in mind, that he narrowed his gaze at his mother, and challenged her preposterous assessment.

"That's ridiculous, Mom. You came up with this theory because I happen to like a woman who I'm not willing to date, for obvious reasons. That happens."

As far as he was concerned, as an employee he supervised, Jennie was off limits for dating. His friends and family all knew that. It was common knowledge Chad wouldn't act on the chemistry that was evident to anyone who spent time around the pair.

"Way off base, Mom."

Chad turned back to the grill and began to scrape again. He felt his mother's eyes watching him but he was finished talking about this. She couldn't be more wrong about him. So, he liked Jennie? He'd liked a lot of women. Some he'd dated and others he hadn't.

Liking Jennie when he couldn't date her didn't mean he was damaged in some way. And it didn't mean he wouldn't date the next woman who came along and caught his eye.

Right?

His eyes found Jennie again, but he forced himself to look away. He really needed to make a point to start seeing someone. His mom might be overbearing at times, but she was right about one thing. It was high time for him to get the hell past Jennie Evans. He'd let this go on way too long already.

CHAPTER 4

*J*ack and Andrew listened as their friend, Peter Mihalik, described the resort property he wanted them to evaluate for him. He was looking to purchase the property from a friend of his family but wanted Jack's and Andrew's opinion of the property as an investment.

"The owner, Jonathan, has carried his nephews for years.," Peter explained as he cut into his steak. "Jonathan's brother and sister-in-law were killed in a car accident when the brothers were twenty and twenty-one. They were a little wild and out of control. They partied a lot, got into a mess of trouble, and brought a lot of stress on the rest of the family. Jonathan had the resort, so he sent them there to run it. It's never been entirely clear to me why he thought that would be a good idea. They're not the brightest guys and I think they're pretty damn lazy. I'm fairly sure the brothers let the managers run the place and they just party and live off their uncle," Peter said with a shrug.

"Why is he looking to sell it now?" Jack asked.

"He's getting older. He also owns Master Blend Winery so his focus has been on wine for years. He doesn't get out to the resort at all anymore. Seems like he wants it out of his hair. Wants the brothers closer to home. I'm pretty sure he'll set them up with a cushy job here. But, if I'm right about them not actually doing any work, despite drawing a salary, and living on the property, then the investment would be a good one. For anyone buying the property, the brothers' salaries would become instant profit. If the general manager wanted to live on the property, she could take over the villa the brothers share," Peter said.

Andrew took a sip of his drink before speaking. "And you want us to look into it for you. See if it's the great buy it looks like it'll be?"

Peter nodded. "If you can. I don't expect you to send anyone out there like you do for your own investments. I was hoping you could look over the paperwork Jonathan sent over. See what you think."

Jack grinned at Andrew and there was a hint of something in his eyes.

"What are you thinking?" Andrew asked Jack.

"That Chad and Jennie could use a vacation," Jack answered before turning to Peter. "You said this resort is mostly for honeymooners and young couples? Can you give us a couple weeks to position ourselves and get back to you?"

Peter looked back and forth between the two of them. "What are you guys plotting?"

"We know a couple that could use a fake honeymoon. I think we'll send two of our team members over there after all. Give us time to have our people take a look. We'll get back to you. In the meantime, can you send me all the financials Jonathan gave you? I can fax a nondisclosure over to you this afternoon," Jack said.

The men shared a few more drinks and caught up over the rest of their meal, but Jack was already scheming in the back of his mind.

He'd watched Jennie and Chad dance around each other for almost a year now. Even though they seemed happy on the outside, he knew they were both missing something in their lives. If he and Andrew could give them the push they needed, to see if there might be more between them than great chemistry, he'd do it. An undercover assignment as honeymooners for two weeks might be just the thing to push those two over the edge.

CHAPTER 5

"Getting too old for this, Jack?" Chad asked his cousin as he, Jack, and Andrew walked off the basketball court after three hours of pickup play.

"You do seem to be limping a little there, Jack," said Andrew, earning a scowl.

"Shut it." Jack lowered himself onto the bleachers beside the court. All three men pulled sweatshirts over damp T-shirts and began exchanging sweaty socks and gym sneakers for dry socks and clean shoes.

Despite the fact they could afford fancy club memberships, all three preferred the pickup games at the local community center gym. They were a lot more fun than the games at the fancy fitness center they'd tried years ago.

"Grab lunch?" Chad asked.

Jack and Andrew both shook their heads.

"I can't. I'm meeting Jill for lunch in an hour. I need to run home and shower," Andrew said.

"I promised Kelly I'd bring her chicken noodle soup from the Daily Grill. She's been craving nothing but chicken noodle soup for a month now." Kelly's pregnancy had been uneventful, with the exception of the cravings that had plagued her—and consequently Jack—since early on.

Jack laughed at Chad's frown. "Hey, get yourself a wife and you won't miss us so much."

"Funny." Chad scowled as the men picked up their bags and started toward the exit.

Jack and Andrew got quiet and Chad groaned inside. He knew what was coming.

Can't everyone drop the whole Jennie and Chad thing?

After picking Jennie up at the park, he had barely managed to get the image of her in a T-shirt with no bra out of his head, and now they had put it front and center again without even mentioning her name.

"Maybe it's time you saw where this thing with Jennie might go. Have you even been on a date with anyone else since you met her?" Jack asked.

They crossed the parking lot toward their cars, but it was clear Jack and Andrew were going to stay until he gave them an answer. Chad didn't want to tell Jack the answer to that question and he didn't want to have this conversation again. As far as they knew, he didn't want to date Jennie because he was her boss at Sutton Capital. And, that was part of it, but Chad hadn't actually told anyone the whole truth.

He opened the door to his truck and threw his gym bag on the passenger seat before turning to face his two best friends. The parking lot was almost empty now and no one was within hearing distance of them. He ran a hand over his jaw and tried to loosen the clenched muscles that had him grinding his teeth together. He didn't succeed.

"Listen guys, I know you mean well, but it's not gonna happen with me and Jennie. It's not just the work thing."

"What do you mean? What other reason could you have for staying away from a woman you're so clearly attracted to?

Everyone knows the feeling's mutual," Andrew said, with a glance at Jack, who nodded.

"Listen, I'll tell you this once and then you guys need to drop it. Got it? Drop it for good. I don't want to keep having this conversation."

Jack and Andrew exchanged looks but then nodded at Chad.

"I did try to see where it would go once. I kissed her. And, it was..." He huffed out a harsh breath at the memory and plowed through his explanation. "It was amazing, just like I knew it would be. But, then I looked in her eyes and all I saw was sorrow. The kind of sorrow that rips you up inside. It killed me to see that look on her face, especially knowing I put it there. I walked away and we haven't talked about it. And we won't. Ever."

He didn't look at his friends. Just kept his eyes on the ground as he leaned on his truck and waited for Jack and Andrew to say something.

"That's ridiculous. Jennie's one of the happiest people I know," Jack said.

Chad understood what Jack meant. They all saw Jennie the way she wanted them to see her. She was brash and saucy and didn't take crap from anyone. She was also always there with a smile or a joke when you needed one.

He looked up to meet his cousin's eyes. "I know how she acts, but I know what I saw. I don't ever want to put that look on her face again and I'm not going to. So drop it, guys. It won't ever happen with me and Jennie."

The day he kissed Jennie, he had known. She wasn't over her husband. She didn't know he knew about the husband. Nobody knew at Sutton. But, he did. He ran the background checks for all of Sutton Capital employees before hiring. He'd been stunned when Jennie's security check had shown she was a widow at such a young age.

He hadn't ever asked her about it and he hadn't shared that part of the report with Jack or Andrew—there hadn't been any reason to. But he suspected the look in her eyes the day he kissed her had a lot to do with her late husband. And, it was a look he never wanted to see again.

"Yeah, okay," Jack said, and then he surprised the hell out of Chad by pulling him into a hug. "I just want you to be happy."

Chad wrapped an arm around Jack's back and squeezed tight. He loved his cousin like a brother.

He pushed back after a minute and shook his head. "You're sweaty and nasty, man. Don't be lovin' on me like that."

Jack huffed out a laugh and shoved Chad back, pushing against his shoulder.

Andrew was shaking his head at them. Chad and Jack exchanged a look and then pulled Andrew into them, smothering him in a sweaty three-way hug. They might be in their thirties, but listening to Andrew fuss as he tried to squirm out from under their onslaught didn't fail to bring a grin to Chad's face.

Jack and Andrew watched Chad pull out of the lot and stood without speaking for a long, drawn out moment. It was Andrew who broke the silence first.

"I think we fucked up."

Jack didn't have to ask what Andrew was talking about. He knew.

He planned to spring the undercover resort job on Chad and Jennie on Monday morning, explaining that the two of them were set up to go undercover as newlyweds for two weeks.

Jack knew Andrew was wondering the same thing he was. Was it really smart to send those two into something like that given what Chad had told them?

"I'll ask Kelly about it. She'll know if it's a good idea or not. We'll leave it up to her. If we need to, I can cancel the plan and just go over the papers Peter sent to help him make a decision."

Andrew nodded, but looked as though his gut were churning over what Chad had just told them, too. Jack wasn't used to feeling unsure. He got the facts, made decisions, and acted. But right now, he was as unsure as he'd ever been. One thing his gut did tell him, though, was that if he made the wrong call here, he could hurt two people he cared about very much.

CHAPTER 6

*J*ennie hopped out of her car, grabbed Zeke's leash, and cut across the lawn to her parents' front door. Since she lived an hour and a half away from them now, she didn't make the trip home every week, but she tried to get there once a month or so.

She let herself in the front door, slipped off Zeke's leash, and called out.

"Mom? Dad? You home?"

She heard a muffled answer from the backyard and made her way through the house and out the screen door to the back patio. There she found not just one set of parents, but two. Kyle's parents, the Evans, still lived next door to Jennie's parents and she still considered them her family. She'd kept Kyle's name after he died so she shared their last name now rather than Davies, her maiden name.

Within minutes, she was surrounded by four pairs of hugging arms pulling her in tight.

Kyle's mother, Anna, spoke first. "We didn't know you were coming! What are you doing here?"

Jennie shrugged and grinned. "Just thought I'd surprise you guys. Maybe stay for the weekend." The truth was, seeing Kelly so close to delivering her baby and Andrew and Jill so happily married had begun to hurt more than Jennie realized it would. She was happy for her friends, but she needed to escape for a bit. She needed to regroup.

Her mom grabbed her in another hug as she spoke to Jennie's dad. "Phil, grab another burger for my baby." To Jennie she said, "We're having burgers and fresh corn on the cob. You picked a perfect night to come home."

Kyle's dad rubbed his round stomach. "And Anna made her peach cobbler."

"Mmmm." Jennie wanted to rub her own tummy at that news. She sat on one of the Adirondack chairs and tucked her feet up under her. It felt good to be home as the two older couples went back to their neighborhood gossip. Who was going to what schools in the fall, and who bought a new ride-on lawnmower.

Jennie sat back and let the chatter about hometown suburbia wash over her like a salve. She sipped the iced tea her mom gave her and watched her dad cook the corn and burgers on the grill.

She didn't have to ask if her mom had made potato salad. Her mother's potato salad was a staple that accompanied anything cooked on the grill in their home. Jennie's mouth watered at the thought of the perfectly cooked red potatoes with bits of diced hardboiled egg and just the right seasonings. She'd tried to make it herself but it never compared to her mom's.

Anna's question brought Jennie out of her quiet thoughts.

"Are you seeing anyone, Jennie?" Anna asked gently.

Jennie's eyes went round. Her parents had given up asking her that long ago but she'd never had the conversation with Kyle's parents. She definitely wasn't prepared for it.

"No! I mean... I don't... No, I'm not." Oh God. Jennie swallowed and looked to her mom, hoping for help. Her mom threw her under the bus instead.

"It's time, Jennie." Her voice was soft but the words cut deeply.

Her father and Kyle's dad stood still, watching but not adding to the conversation as Jennie shook her head at the two women. She lowered her head and stared at the patio stones beneath her chair.

How do I explain that it won't ever be time? Kyle is dead. There won't be a time when that changes and there won't be a time when I'm ready to replace him. Ever.

Jennie could practically feel the looks they were all exchanging but she couldn't bring herself to look at them. She didn't want to see the expectation there. Didn't want to see the shock. Naturally, after four years, anyone would expect her to move on. Even her husband's own parents.

They didn't understand. They couldn't. No one but Jennie knew the real reason Kyle had died. And no one ever would.

Jennie kept her head down and waited. Eventually, the chatter began again and the topic was dropped. For now.

But, she feared her biggest source of respite, her source of comfort and understanding, was about to be lost. How could she hide here, when the pain followed her home?

CHAPTER 7

*J*ack stood in the doorway to the living room watching Kelly sleep, watching the movement of her chest as it rose and fell with each breath.

Whether awake or asleep, the sight of his wife stole his breath and made him want to sink to his knees. How close he'd come to losing her...and now, not only did he have her, but they had their daughter on the way...

Jack didn't know how the hell he'd gotten so damn lucky, but he'd never be complacent. He thanked whatever powers were watching over them every day, for Kelly and their baby.

She wasn't sleeping well at night anymore. Lately, Kelly would sleep for a few hours at night before Jack heard her climb out of bed and haunt the lower floors of the house. The doctor said that was normal this late in a pregnancy but it killed Jack to see her so worn out. He turned from the doorway, planning to let her rest but she called to him. He turned to find Kelly's eyes on him and a sleepy smile on her face.

"I didn't mean to wake you, sweetheart. You should sleep." He crossed to her and sat on the edge of the couch with her, then ran the back of his hand down the soft skin on her face.

"It's okay. I've been asleep for a few hours. If I sleep any longer, I'll be up all night for sure."

He laid a hand on his wife's rounded belly. "How's our girl today?"

They hadn't agreed on a name yet. In the mix were Madeleine, Lacey and Hadley. But, the mix tended to change daily.

Kelly pulled herself up and Jack propped a few pillows behind her on the couch. Once she was settled in, he figured it was as good a time as any to bring up the subject of Jennie and Chad.

Jack wasn't sure how to ask his wife about her best friend. "Hey, Kelly? Did something ever happen to Jennie that would make her avoid dating?"

"What do you mean?" Kelly asked, looking like she had an idea but didn't want to talk about it.

"Chad told Andrew and me he kissed Jennie once and she got a really sad look on her face, so he never tried anything again. I always thought it was only the work thing keeping them apart, but he says there's more to it."

"Oh, no."

Jack knew by the tone in Kelly's voice and the look on her face that she knew what was going on with Jennie. "Oh, God. I had no idea anything happened between them. She never said anything."

He was confused but waited for Kelly to continue.

"Jennie was married before, Jack. She's a widow."

"What? How could we not know that? How is that possible? In fact, I know it's not possible. We do background checks on employees. We would have seen it." Jack was shaking his head but Kelly looked so certain.

"Do you see all the background checks?"

"No. I guess not. Chad checks them and he usually gives me a quick okay or tells me if there's an issue." Understanding swept over him. "Chad must know. It must have shown up in her report, but he would have respected her privacy. He'd keep that private, even from me, since she never volunteered the information herself and it wasn't relevant to her working for us. I can't believe she's a widow. She's so young. What happened? When?" His mind ran over everything he knew about the seemingly happy woman who had started out as his temporary secretary, but was now a friend.

"They grew up together. Fell in love in high school and somehow managed to stay together even through college." Kelly smiled. "It was a fairytale love but it ended in tragedy. They were married for a year when he died from cancer. That was four years ago, but she hasn't gotten over it. She dates men from time to time, but honestly, they're more like friends that take her to dinner. I think she doesn't truly want to find someone else. I have a feeling Chad challenges that reluctance for her. I think she feels a lot more for Chad than she wants to. If she looked upset, my guess is it had to do with feelings she's not ready to have."

Jack scrubbed his hands down his face. He was trying to rub away the confusion and figure out how to tell his wife what he'd done.

"I think Andrew and I screwed up, honey," he began, feeling more out of his element than he had in a long time. Uneasy wasn't an emotion he was used to.

Kelly was watching him with apprehension. She put a hand on his face and rubbed his jaw softly with her thumb. "What did you do?"

"A friend of mine wanted my opinion on a resort property in the Florida Keys he wants to buy. It's a high-end place that caters mostly to young couples, honeymooners, that type of thing. I told Peter I'd send someone to check it out, see if anything comes up. Andrew and I arranged for Chad and Jennie to go in as honeymooners on Monday. They, uh... They don't know yet. We're planning to tell them it came up suddenly. We thought it would be a good way to give them a little push, you know?"

"Can you cancel it?" Kelly sat up further, looking a lot more alert than she had moments before.

"Absolutely. I can look over the numbers for my friend, and do an assessment for him without sending anyone out there. If you think that's what I should do, I'll do it in a heartbeat," he assured her.

Jack watched Kelly as she seemed to struggle with the decision.

"It's all right, Kels. I'll go cancel it. I shouldn't have done it in the first place." Jack started to stand, but Kelly put a hand on his arm to stop him.

"No," she said slowly. "I'll probably go to hell for this, but maybe you should send them. I think Jennie's been sad, watching all of us getting married, seeing us start a family. I know something's got her stuck in the past, but maybe it would be good to see if we can nudge her out of it."

Jack's eyebrows just about shot through the roof. "You think I should send them?"

Kelly nodded. "If it was anyone other than Chad, I'd say no. But, they're adults and we can trust Chad. If Jennie doesn't want anything to happen, nothing will. He won't pressure her. But, if I'm right about her feelings for him, maybe he can help her get past whatever's been holding her back."

"You're sure?" Jack asked.

"No. Not at all." She looked positively miserable at the idea that she might be doing the wrong thing for Jennie.

Jack wrapped his arms around her. "You're right about one thing, though. We can trust Chad with her. If Jennie doesn't want anything to happen, nothing will."

Kelly was quiet for a few more minutes.

"Text me when you tell them Monday and I'll call Jennie and see how she's doing. If she's totally freaked, you can make an excuse and say it's cancelled. If she's okay, we let them go. Sound good?"

Jack nodded and began to rain kisses down his wife's jaw line, across her neck, to her shoulder. Before he could get much further, Kelly gasped and sat straight up – well, as straight up as her pregnant belly would allow.

"Wait! If you're sending Jennie away for two weeks, she might not be here when the baby's born. We can't do that. She needs to be here, Jack."

He smiled at his wife, pushing her back on the pillows and continuing his slow caress of the body he loved.

"The doctor said most women don't go into labor early their first time." He smiled at Kelly as she whimpered in response to his statement. He knew she was dying to have the baby on time, not wanting to be pregnant a moment past her due date.

"Commercial flight time is only about two and half hours but I promise to have a jet on standby. She won't wait at the airport or anything. We'll whisk her out of there and get her home in an hour, an hour and a half, tops. She won't miss the delivery. I promise."

Kelly laid back down and grinned at him, as he went back to worshiping the woman who was about to make him the happiest daddy in the world.

CHAPTER 8

*J*ennie sat in the comfortable seat in first class but she was anything but comfortable. Her head had been spinning since that morning when Jack gave her and Chad a new assignment.

She'd barely had time to go home and pack for the two-week-long trip, let alone think about what it would mean to be pretending to be Chad's wife in a tropical resort set up for romance and seduction.

When Jack first explained the assignment to them, she'd had a flash of panic, but there was no way she'd refuse an assignment from him. She loved her work at Sutton Capital and wouldn't jeopardize it even though going through with this particular job terrified her.

After Kyle died, Jennie had floundered for quite some time, bouncing from one temporary job to the next. The truth was, she hadn't had much interest in 'finding her way' as her parents had encouraged her to. She had just wanted to get by.

That changed when Jack took her on as a permanent member of his security and investigations staff. She had no idea why Jack took a chance on her the way he did. As his temporary assistant she had overstepped her job description and could have been fired for listening in on Jack's private conversations.

But, her eavesdropping had ended up helping Jack out and Jack Sutton never did anything conventional.

She liked the work. Really liked it. The only downside had been her insane attraction to Chad, but she'd managed to keep her walls up with him. She made sure she kept him at arm's length at all times and didn't let their interactions get past superficial conversation and impertinent jokes.

And yet, somehow, they did get closer. Despite her best efforts, she knew Chad saw through her. And there was the one time she'd made a mistake and let him get too close. He kissed her and nearly brought her to her knees. For one sweet incredible moment, she forgot about Kyle. Forgot the hurt. The pain. The loss. The guilt.

And then the kiss broke and the realization had hit. How could she let another man make her forget? How could she do that to Kyle? Hadn't she done enough to him already?

Jennie chanced a glance at Chad. He'd been even more quiet than usual through the whole morning. He hadn't said much of anything in Jack's office, though she'd felt his eyes on her, assessing her reaction. He picked her up at her house and carried her bags to the car, all without a word. He spoke as little as possible as they drove Zeke over to Jill and Andrew's house, where he would stay for the two weeks she and Chad were at the resort.

And now, he sat silent, by her side. Usually she hated it when he was this quiet. It made her want to fill the silence and when she did, she ended up babbling, spewing verbal diarrhea all over the damn place.

But, Jennie didn't feel much like talking right now.

Two weeks pretending to be in love with Chad. *How will I do this? Never mind 'do this' – how will I survive it?*

She bit down on her lip and looked out the plane's window.

She felt like crying. Then Chad took her hand and squeezed. He leaned in to whisper in her ear.

"Don't worry, Jennie. We can do this."

That was it. That's all he said and then he leaned back and fell asleep in his chair. But he didn't let go of her hand. And she didn't let go either.

Chad began to relax as he listened to Jennie babble to the driver on their way from the airport to the resort. She didn't let the driver's limited ability with English stop her. She chatted on and on like a little songbird. This was Jennie in her undercover persona and Chad was happy to see her there.

He felt a grin crack his face for the first time since he'd walked into Jack's office that morning. Watching Jennie in work mode always made him laugh because no one ever saw her coming. She would have made a brilliant actress.

At the moment, she was telling the driver about a pattern she'd found to crochet a baby yoda costume for her dog and how she was planning to learn to crochet just so she could make it.

When Jennie went undercover, she acted like a complete airhead. It was what made her so good at their work. She could befriend everyone and most people assumed she was a total idiot, the way she prattled on about anything and everything.

And because they believed she was the ditzy girl she portrayed, they spoke freely to her and in front of her. Jennie, who was anything but an airhead, soaked it all in, remembering every detail. She knew when to prod further and when to back off.

When they teamed up together, the effect was even better. With his size, most people assumed he was a giant meathead. As long as Chad stayed quiet and let them think that, people had the same habit of speaking freely in front of him.

When he and Jennie worked together, it was usually just a matter of putting themselves in the right places to overhear conversations and observe a business's day-to-day operations. It was an unorthodox approach, to say the least, but it worked. If there were any weaknesses in a company, they found them.

The driver pulled into the circular entrance of the sprawling main building of the resort. A smiling doorman came forward to open their doors and load luggage onto a polished brass, rolling cart. Chad took Jennie's hand to help her out of the car and watched her face as she took in the gorgeous white stone building with its terra cotta roof and ornate open-air entryway.

The sight of her still took his breath away. He saw her almost every damn day at work or out on the weekends with his friends, but it didn't seem to lessen the impact she had on him. Every time Chad looked at Jennie's peaches and cream skin with the dusting of light freckles across her nose and the tops of her cheeks, he felt like he'd been punched in the gut. He wanted to lose himself in the long strands of her wild hair, its crazy straw-berry-blond curls tangling in his fingers as he pulled her in to taste her mouth. The mouth he couldn't forget after just one kiss.

She looked at him and grinned, snapping him back to reality. A reality where Jennie Evans would never be his.

"Remind me to thank Jack." Then she leaned in close so only he would hear, the proximity sending him back into fantasy land. "I can't believe we're getting paid for this. Two weeks in heaven."

Heaven? Nah. This is going to be two weeks in hell, Jennie girl. Two weeks in fucking hell pretending to have what he never would.

Chad put his hand on Jennie's waist, pulling her close and walking with her into the lobby. There, they were greeted by another staff member who offered them flutes of champagne. Jack had apparently booked a very high-end package for them because they never even made it to the front desk. They were greeted by name and shown immediately to a secluded villa on the beach.

Chad would have preferred to be a little less obtrusive. He'd learned it pays to blend in with the masses and not stand out like a sore thumb when you're trying to gather information. If he'd planned this trip, he would have chosen a room that was in the middle of the price range with the right number of amenities to allow them to conform to that of most of the people there.

But Jack had planned this job without a word to Chad before this morning. And that seemed damn suspicious to Chad. He had a feeling his cousin was up to something, but he tried to put that thought aside. Jack certainly wouldn't be stupid enough to send Chad and Jennie here for anything other than innocent, work-related reasons. Not after what Chad had told Jack and Andrew over the weekend.

Would he?

CHAPTER 9

Thankfully, once they began moving, Chad released his hold on her waist. Jennie needed space to salvage the remaining bits of her wits.

She tried to lose herself in thoughts of work as they walked to the private villa on the beach. She couldn't believe she would share this retreat with Chad for the next two weeks.

The resort was hot and tropical, filled with the sounds of birds and the ocean with a light breeze that teased over her skin. Even the air smelled different here.

They followed the woman who'd introduced herself as Maria when she'd greeted them in the lobby. They went past the common areas and crossed into an area of dense shrubs and trees, following a small sandy path through the growth. When they emerged moments later, their private villa stood in front of them. It was surrounded by the finest white sand Jennie had ever walked on. She took off her sandals and held onto Chad's arm as they crossed the warm sand to the porch at the front of the villa.

If touching the smooth, hard muscles of Chad's arm hadn't stolen Jennie's breath already, the view certainly would have. They faced the ocean with its crystal-blue water. There was a teak double chaise lounge on the front porch filled with soft pillows, and a hammock off to one side. Sail boats provided a bright splash of color on the pale blue sky.

Jennie gasped when she stepped inside the villa. The house looked like a tiny grass hut from the outside but it was anything but that. It was smothered in luxury and comfort.

"It's beautiful!" She didn't know what to look at first. The doors and furniture were made of a beautiful dark wood with ornate carvings and patterns. The chairs and couch looked comfortable and inviting. A small fireplace in the corner promised a real honeymooning couple romantic evenings if the temperature dropped at night. Overhead fans made to look like big leaves turned lazily throughout the room to stir the hot air.

Jennie walked through the living room to large double doors that opened to an enormous master bedroom. In fact, thinking back to the doors she'd seen as she walked through, and the size of the villa from the outside, Jennie had a sneaking suspicion this was the only bedroom. Their bags had already been placed in the room by the hotel staff and the bed was covered in pastel rose petals and towels intricately folded to look like a bouquet of flowers.

That's right. This is the honeymoon villa.

Try as she might, Jennie couldn't keep from imagining Chad laying her on the bed, his strong body coming down over her. His heated hands and mouth...

She heard Chad approach and felt his presence behind her a minute later. She turned to see him leaning on the door jamb, hands shoved in his pockets, his bad boy grin firmly in place on his face.

"Big bed," he said, peering around her.

Jennie laughed at Chad, but on the inside, she felt her body grow hot in response to his presence in the room, to his suggestive tone. It was a battle to steady her breathing instead of letting her body run wild with its response to him.

"It's all yours, Boss Man. I'll be sleeping on the couch."

That got Chad's attention and he stood and stepped toward her. His no nonsense boss tone was back. "You're not sleeping on the couch, Jen. I was joking about the bed. I'll be on the couch. You're in here."

"Don't be silly, Chad. I'm a foot shorter than you. I'll be fine out on the couch or even on one of the chaise lounge chairs. Hell, any of them look more comfy than my bed at home. Comfy for a person my size, not yours." She gave him a pointed look as she finished. There was no way he'd be comfortable on a couch at his size. It was ridiculous to even think of doing things his way.

Chad let out something between a growl and a laugh. "Not happening, Jennie." He crossed the room to grab his bag and headed to the living room.

"You can't do that, Chad. We're married, remember? You need to keep your clothes in here or the housekeepers will wonder what you did to land yourself in the doghouse when we've only been married a couple of days."

He looked at her for a long minute. She could see the tension in his jaw as he fought against what he wanted and what they had to pretend to be for the next two weeks.

Without a word, he crossed to the dresser and closet and began to unpack his clothes. Jennie sat on the bed and watched him, amused.

As one might expect from someone who'd spent so many years in the military, everything had its place in Chad's world. He lined his extra shoes along the bottom of the closet. He folded clothes and organized them in different drawers. Hung dress shirts and pants on hangers and arranged them with precisely one inch between each hanger.

Jennie followed him into the bathroom and watched him set out his toiletries, lining up toothbrush, toothpaste, brush, and razor just so. He left the same distance between each item on the counter.

Chad eyed her as he walked back out of the bathroom. He

scooped up the flip flops she had kicked off at the foot of the bed and walked out to the front of the villa. Jennie padded after him and stifled a giggle when he lined up her flip flops by the door. He slipped off the sneakers he had on and lined them up next to her shoes.

Apparently satisfied, he began taking extra pillows off the couch.

Oh, this is too good to resist.

Jennie went to the small bar in the living room and opened a can of soda for herself.

"Want one?" she asked Chad, holding up the can.

"No thanks. I'll probably go to sleep soon. I wasn't planning on such a long day of travel and I was up half the night getting a few reports ready for Jack."

"You didn't know about this trip ahead of time?" She frowned.

He shook his head. "Not a clue. I found out about it the same time you did."

She paused mid sip and looked at him. "Isn't that weird? I mean, don't you usually plan these things? If you didn't plan it, who did?" She'd had been so busy trying to convince herself she could do this job when they'd been in Jack's office earlier, she hadn't even looked at Chad to see if he looked surprised. Now she had to wonder if he was as thrown as she was.

While she waited for his reply, she walked over to the front door and slipped her feet in her flip flops. She walked back to the couch, sat down next to Chad, kicked her flip flops off, and curled her feet up under her on the couch.

"Jack and Andrew planned this one on their own. I think it was pretty last minute. The friend that asked for a favor went to school with them so I think they wanted to help the guy out." As Chad spoke, he eyed Jennie's shoes on the floor beneath them.

She smiled her most innocent smile as she watched Chad size up her shoes. He stood and picked them up again and put them back by the door before coming back to the couch.

Oh my God. I had no idea he was such a neat freak.

"Jack's sending us info to look over tomorrow. He emailed and said Peter sent financials earlier and there are a few areas we need to look into. Something about the boating trips and scuba diving," Chad said. "That's all I know for now."

Jennie popped up off the couch and wandered to the kitchen. "I wonder if they have snacks in here." She began opening and closing cabinets and the fridge and calling off anything she found.

"Bottled water. More sodas. No snacks. Hmmmm. We should stock up on late night snacks." She walked back to the front door, slipped her shoes on, and wandered back to the bedroom.

"We pick up the phone any time we want anything and have it sent, Jennie," Chad said and she could hear the smile in his voice as he spoke.

She came back into the room carrying her toothbrush and kicked her shoes off at the marble-topped table in the kitchen before plopping into one of the chairs.

"But, what if I just want popcorn in the middle of the night?"

Chad laughed and shook his head. "They'll get you anything you want, any time. Day or night. It's that kind of place and I'm pretty sure Jack booked us that kind of package. He seems to have gone with premium everything. We don't have to lift a finger for the next two weeks. Might as well enjoy it."

"Huh. Nice. All right. I'm hittin' the shower, Big Man." Jennie popped up again and began to cross the room but kept one eye on the room behind her.

Sure enough, the second she stepped away from her shoes, Chad crossed the room to put them back by the door again. Jennie turned and watched him.

When he returned to the couch, he lay down and closed his eyes. He put his feet up on one arm of the couch and his head on a pillow he'd braced across the other arm.

She tiptoed over to the front door and raised her foot to slip into the flip flops once again.

"Whaaaaa!" Jennie squealed as Chad wrapped a strong arm around her waist. He lifted her off the floor before she could get so much as a toe into her shoe.

Laughing, she squeaked as he walked to the bathroom with her locked in place. "Put me down!"

She heard Chad's low laugh and felt the rumbling it brought to his chest. God, he felt so damn good she wanted to cry.

And he smelled good, too. Spicy clean and manly.

He dropped her to her feet in the bathroom and shut the door.

"Good night, Jen," she heard through the door.

By that time, the laughter had left her system, replaced by heat. She'd felt pure lust spread through her traitorous body when she was pressed against the hard expanse of Chad's chest and the flat chiseled muscles of his stomach.

She'd wanted to grind against him, pressing her hips back into him as she did. She'd wanted to spin in his arms and wrap herself around him to kiss him senseless. As she stood in the bathroom without him, she could think only one thing: she wanted that strong arm wrapped around her again, holding her tight, hugging her to him. Wanted and didn't want...all in one breath.

CHAPTER 10

"Hey Jack, what ya got for us?" Chad asked as he and Jennie sat on opposite sides of his phone, which was set on speaker. Between the size of the couch and the temptation of Jennie in the room next to him, Chad hadn't slept well at all.

Touching her last night had been a mistake. Wrapping one arm around her for the brief minute it took to move her to the bathroom before she could get to her flip flops again was all it took to have Chad stirred up.

He now knew how she would feel as she writhed beneath him. Knew how soft her body felt against his. How she brought the temperature up with just that slight connection. How she would feel as he pressed his body into hers, holding her tight for one agonizing thrust after another as he drove them both over the brink.

And that knowledge had tormented him all damned night.

"Did you get the financials I emailed?" came Jack's reply, whipping Chad back to reality.

"Yes. We looked them over this morning," he glanced at Jennie. "I think we need a little more guidance here. We don't know what to look for."

"I figured you might. It's a weird situation. The resort is owned by Jonathan Masters, owner of Master Blend Winery. His winery focuses on inexpensive blends of wine marketed as everyday table wine. You've probably seen it."

"Yeah, it's in just about every grocery store and liquor store in the United States," Jennie said. "The one with the skinny old guy with a pipe and glasses leaning into a huge barrel of wine on the label."

Jack laughed. "That's the one. And, in fact, that's a caricature of Jonathan Masters. He's now in his seventies and rarely spends time at the resort. He has no interest in running it. He's left his two nephews, Matt and Alan Masters, running it for him for the last few years, but he's looking to get out. My friend Peter is thinking of buying it but he's a little unclear as to how well those nephews have been running the place. Peter has known the Masters family for a long time and always got the sense that the nephews were pretty lazy."

"We can try to track them down today and check them out," Chad said.

"Good. See if you can find out if they're really running things or if the managers are running it and the nephews are taking a salary just for sitting on their asses. It seems like the place is a little heavy on managers if, in fact, the nephews are working. If they're token employees, their salaries would disappear and turn into instant profit for Peter" said Jack.

Jennie shrugged and looked at Chad. "Should be easy to find out. I'll get close to them," she said with a grin.

Chad rolled his eyes, but on the inside, he seethed at the idea of her getting close to any man other than him.

Jack continued, obviously unaware of Chad's feelings on the matter. "I'm also confused about how they're running money through the business out there. The marina is operated by a separate company. It's an independent contractor that runs fishing boats, kayak rentals, scuba diving trips, and that kind of thing from the two docks at the resort. The setup is odd, though."

They listened as Jack explained his concerns. "The resort collects all the fees for the services and rentals and then pays the money out to the contractor, taking a percentage. It's an odd way to set up the system rather than simply leasing the docks and beach area to the company for a monthly fee. It makes a lot of extra work for the front desk people to book things that way. My hunch is the nephews don't know any better and the marina company is taking advantage of them. If that's the case, Peter can change the setup if he buys the place, but I want to be sure. Can you snoop around and see what you can find out?"

"You got it," Chad said.

"Okay. In the meantime, I'll find out who owns the company that runs the marina," Jack said.

"Anything else?" Chad asked.

"Yeah, how's the villa?"

"It's horrible, Jack. I expect hazard pay for these two weeks," Jennie said, laughing.

"Wise ass," came Jack's unorthodox reply. None of them really had a traditional employer and employee relationship at this point. Jennie was more like a sister to Jack now, than someone who worked for him.

"I'll tell Kelly you're having the vacation of a lifetime," Jack said.

"We'll call when we have something, Jack," Chad laughed as he hit the button to end the call.

As Jennie and Chad came off the secluded pathway that connected their villa to the more populated area of the resort, he reached down and took her hand in his.

"Where do you want to eat, hon?" He asked Jennie. There

were several choices of restaurants in the resort, all included in the price of the package. Guests didn't need to bring their wallets anywhere for food or drink.

"Casual for breakfast and lunch, fancy for dinners?" Jennie asked. He recognized her proposal for what it was. She was stepping into their negotiation mode. He and Jennie had a shorthand way of cutting deals and agreeing on things when they were on assignment. Sometimes the negotiations were easy. Other times, they butted heads and their negotiation became real.

He made a face. "We're on vacation. No fancy dinners."

In a move she'd never employed in their negotiations before —and which Chad had to attribute to the fact they were posing as newlyweds, since Jennie was always very careful to keep space between them and avoid any unnecessary touching—she turned and pressed her full body against his. He felt her soft thighs, gorgeous hips, and those irresistible breasts of hers press against his hard body. He gritted his teeth to resist her pull, but he couldn't completely prevent his body's response.

Hell. Two weeks in hell.

She went up on tiptoes, brushing her body against his with that witchy, captivating smile on her face that she always got when she was being playful. He stood stock-still. She whispered in his ear, her hot, sweet mouth so close to his. He thought for a brief second about turning his head to capture it in a searing kiss, but he knew he'd pay for it if he did.

Not because she'd do anything, but because it would bring him to all new levels of pain. If he kissed her again, his body would be wound so tight and hard, he wouldn't be able to manage the walk across the resort.

"Please," was all she whispered but the damage was done and she knew it. She smiled and winked at him, knowing she'd won that round. As Jennie turned and walked toward one of the restaurants, he smacked her in the ass.

If she was going to change her tactics on this trip, so was he.

She squealed and took a few running steps to get ahead of him. Shit, he could work with that, too. He hung back and enjoyed the view all the way to breakfast.

Jennie Evans in a skirt and sandals was a sight to behold.

CHAPTER 11

*F*our days into their trip, Jennie and Chad had a good sense of the layout of the resort and it was already clear the nephews did little to run the place. So far, they'd seen them flirting with guests, drinking all day, and playing golf.

They schmoozed with some of the guests, but that was about the extent of it. They didn't even seem to engage with the managers much. From everything Chad had seen, they let the managers run the show.

It took everything Chad had in him not to go caveman when Jennie was talking to the Masters brothers. In classic Jennie style, she simply swam over to them at the swim up bar and started flirting.

They were buying her drinks in no time and she was doing her airhead routine. By the time she signaled Chad to come break up the party and get her out of there—which he gladly did, playing the role of the jealous meathead husband—she'd found out a lot about the brothers.

They didn't lift a damn finger. They liked to play the big shots, even going so far as to refer to the resort as 'their' resort. They soaked up the sun and played and took credit for the resort's success, but that was it.

When Jennie put on those big doe eyes and twirled a finger through her hair, saying how hard it must be to run the place, they laughed. They looked around and shrugged their shoulders and said, "This is it. We're free to play with you all day."

Today, she and Chad were trying to figure out more about the marina. There were a lot of extra activities guests could purchase at the resort. Everything from swimming with dolphins, to a trip to a national park or a four-day fishing trip, and more.

Every afternoon, the representatives from the different tour agencies were in the lobby, signing people up for excursions. You signed up with the tour company of your choice, paid the representative directly, and booked a date for your activity.

For everything except the marina. For the marina, you spoke to the tour representative to choose an activity and book a date, but then they gave you a slip to take to the front desk where you paid for your tour.

So far, Jennie and Chad hadn't been able to pick up on a reason for that additional step. If need be, Jack would flat out ask the owner why things were done this way, but they liked to try to get a sense of things on their own sometimes first.

It was amazing the things they found out when Jennie and Chad went into some of the companies they looked at.

Just three weeks before, Jennie had gone into a company and in less than a week discovered that the medical research the company promised was about to revolutionize diabetes treatment had already been proven to be a bust, internally.

The owners thought they could get funding from Jack based on the outdated early findings and use that funding to buy more time to make new discoveries and hopefully come out on top.

The sad thing was, if they'd been up front with Jack, he might have given them money anyway. Their ideas were promising and they had a few things in the early stages that people in the medical field Jack consulted with thought were promising. But the fact that they were trying to pull one over on Sutton Capital, instead of being upfront, killed their chances for good.

With any luck, Jennie would work her magic here and figure out if the resort owner or its management had anything to hide.

The resort had two docks. One where the fishing boats and the boats taking guests scuba diving docked. The other was in a small bay where guests could snorkel and go out in kayaks.

Chad and Jennie were over in the bay, sitting on the edge of the dock as they put on snorkels and masks. They'd decided to skip the flippered feet and just swim around leisurely close to the beach.

"Twenty-seven kayaks," Jennie said absently as she fidgeted with her mask.

"What?" Chad asked.

Jennie shrugged a shoulder. "I was counting the slots for kayaks," she said, pointing to the racks that held the kayaks on the side of the bay. "Looks like all but five are out right now, assuming they actually fill all of the slots. I suppose they may have fewer kayaks than the number of slots for kayaks, though."

Chad let her talk. He was used to this. She just catalogued sometimes. They were both observant, which made them really good at their jobs. But they each observed different things.

Chad watched people. Their movements and body language. Facial expressions, ticks, and tells. He watched their surroundings, always knowing how to get them out of a situation if he needed to.

Not that they needed that in the work they did now. They didn't do anything dangerous for Sutton. In fact, their version of 'undercover' was using their real names, and pretending to be less intelligent than they were.

Chad's situational awareness was a habit left over from his military tours. He doubted it was something he would ever have to use again. It was something that was so ingrained at this point, it was simply a part of who he was. He had noted the small motor boat tied to the dock because it was a means to escape the area.

Jennie was different. She counted things and noticed details he didn't. She could tell you if someone wore fake designer clothes or if they were the real deal. She could tell you who designed a person's shoes and, sometimes, whether their jewelry was real or paste. And, for some unknown reason, things like the number of kayaks caught her eye.

Actually, if he thought about it, he could guess why she'd noticed the kayaks. Their bright colors. Jennie surrounded herself with bright, happy colors.

The outside of her house was a light cheerful yellow. He hadn't been inside her house, though he'd dropped her off or picked her up a few times. But he would guess the inside would be filled with color as well.

The kayaks were bright red and orange. She would like those colors.

"Come on," Chad grinned at her. She looked adorable with goggles covering almost half her face. "Let's go see some fish."

They jumped in the water and lowered masked faces into the bay.

Before Chad knew what hit him, he heard a shriek and had an armful of sputtering Jennie. She quite literally climbed up him and was clinging to his shoulders, legs and arms clamped around him as high up as she could go. It would be funny to anyone watching.

Chad grinned, trying to ignore his body's immediate response to her. He refused to acknowledge the fact that at that moment, the string bikini she wore was giving him access to parts of Jennie's body he'd only ever dreamed of touching. His arms were under her ass, holding her up. The sensations produced by their wet skin were wreaking havoc on his senses, but she didn't seem to be aware of that at all.

"Problem, Jen?"

She bit her lip and nodded her head.

"And that would be...?" *Damn, she's cute.* On any other woman, this would seem like a coy ploy for his attention. With Jennie, it was real. She was well and truly freaked by something and he was more than happy to be her knight in shining armor. Especially when she wrapped her body around that armor.

"The fish," Jennie said, eyes wide. "A fish touched my legs. It went right between my legs!"

He let a slow smile form. "I need to protect you from the fish?"

She nodded. "They're huge. And scary. And kind of gross."

They were pretty big. Some of them were one-and-a-half feet long and about as wide around the middle as Chad's forearm. He had expected smaller fish, too. But seeing her so freaked out was pretty damned cute.

And holding her was pretty sexy. Really, really damned sexy, as a matter of fact. Chad lifted her up to the dock, then let his hands skim down to her thighs—pretending to be Jennie's concerned husband did have its perks.

"Want me to hold you in the water and see if that makes you feel better?" *Say yes. No, say no. This is a bad idea... But, please say yes.*

Before Jennie could answer, a fish jumped out of the water and splashed back in. Chad assumed it was trying to catch a bug skimming the surface of the water. Jennie must have assumed it was an attempt to eat her, because she was up and running off the dock in a heartbeat. So much for Jack's theory that Jennie Evans wasn't afraid of anything.

Chad pulled himself out onto the dock, trying not to laugh too hard—and losing that battle. He scooped up their beach bag and towels. The items quickly became crucial parts of Chad's ensemble as he followed Jennie back to the villa.

Watching the sway of her sweet ass as she hightailed it through the resort had his dick harder than he'd care to share with the other guests. With their belongings held casually in front of him to hide his predicament, he let himself enjoy the show. He'd have to shower with ice water when he got back to the villa, but it was worth it.

Jennie had the sexiest ass Chad had ever seen. That ass in a bikini?

Deadly.

CHAPTER 12

*T*he first week of their working vacation passed fairly quickly. They stuck to the pools instead of the ocean so Jennie didn't have any more run-ins with the terrifying fish of the Florida coast. And they kept an eye out for the nephews.

Jack wasn't in any hurry for their assessment and rarely checked in with them. That struck Jennie as a little odd, but she brushed it off. She and Chad were having more fun than she thought they would. They spent their days in the resort where she managed to befriend a few of the employees.

Most of the employees seemed to feel that the Masters brothers didn't have much to offer. They were careful not to badmouth them too much, but Jennie didn't miss the undertone of what people weren't saying. No one respected the brothers. The brothers were dead weight on the resort and none of the employees would be sorry to see them go.

People liked and spoke well of Jonathan Masters, the owner, but they said he rarely came there anymore. From what Jennie could see, the managers were running the show and, it seemed, running it very well. The place had an incredibly relaxing atmosphere with attention to detail and customer service that left guests feeling pampered. It was exactly what a tropical vacation should be.

At night, they went to dinner and then played cards or talked and laughed back in the villa. They talked and laughed a lot, actually. More than she had thought they would.

Even though it was hard to ignore the sexual undertones that always sparked between them, Jennie really enjoyed being with Chad on this new level.

The night before, they had gone to one of the restaurants that had dinner and dancing. Jennie was stunned to find out Chad could salsa, rumba—you name it, he could do it on the dance floor. As he whirled her around, making her breathless, she had to laugh. She never would have pictured her tough soldier-man boss as a dancer.

"Where did you learn to do this?" she had asked when they sat down for their entrees.

He shrugged a shoulder and grinned at her. "I have my secrets."

She shook her head at him, to which he'd just winked.

"If I tell you, I'll have to kill you."

She stuck her tongue out at him.

This afternoon, they lay in lounge chairs by one of the pools, pretending to be a couple in love. They were fairly sure they had found out all they needed to know about the Masters brothers. They'd booked a boat tour the next day to see if they could find out more about the marina and how it functioned. For now, there was nothing to do but relax.

"Hey, Boss Man," Jennie said, cracking her eyes open to peek at Chad while she swirled her empty drink at him. "Wanna swim over to the bar and get me another daiquiri?"

After three strawberry daiquiris, she was a little tipsy. She was probably being a little too uppity with her boss, even for her, but they had both let down their guard quite a bit.

He lowered his sunglasses and leaned over her on the lounge

chair. His body almost entirely covered hers and his face was right in hers. She could feel the heat coming off of him, and damn if that didn't go straight to her legs.

Well, not her legs. Between her legs, really. Right where it counted. His mouth was an inch from hers and she had to fight not to reach up and close the distance. Not to see what would happen if she simply gave in to temptation and tasted that mouth.

When he spoke, he cranked her body heat up without any effort at all. "Now, Jen, what will people think if they hear you call me Boss Man?" he asked quietly.

She licked her lips. "That we're into kink and role playing?"

As usual, the sexy rumble of his voice when he spoke so softly to her sent her body spiraling out of control. She itched to reach out and touch his chest. It was hot and tanned and just a little sweaty from the searing Florida sun. She knew it would feel heavenly under her fingertips, the hard cut of the muscles under the satiny taut skin.

She didn't notice the tiny moan that slipped from her lips until it was too late to stop it.

She saw Chad's eyes burn hot and dark for a second. Her breath caught at the intensity in his eyes and she felt his whole body coil and tense above her.

And then he pulled back. Jennie watched as he slid into the water and cut clean strokes across the pool to the swim up bar. She let out a breath she hadn't realized she was holding and groaned.

That was stupid. How did that cliché go? She was playing with fire and she was going to get burned? Yeah, that she believed.

One more week.

CHAPTER 13

$\mathcal{T}$wo other couples waited on the dock when Chad and Jennie arrived for their boat tour. They would be going to a quiet bay to swim—although he expected Jennie to stay in the boat for that given her fear of the fish. After that, they'd go to a quaint restaurant along the coast for lunch, and later tour a local market where they could shop for local touristy junk, before being taken back to the resort.

Jennie stood with the small group and began to do her chit chatty thing while Chad sat on one of the benches and watched her. She had on a red bikini and a brightly patterned wrap tied around her waist. She leaned her head back and laughed at something one of the other couples said and Chad couldn't resist.

He reached out and looped an arm around her waist, pulling her down onto his lap. She yelped while the other women cooed over his romantic gesture. One woman swatted her husband on the arm and scowled at him.

"You never treat me like that anymore," she said, drawing a laugh from the group.

"They're newlyweds," her husband said. That earned him another whack.

Chad could barely pay attention. His arms were around

Jennie's bare waist. Her skin was so soft and smooth. It was silky and creamy and it begged for his touch. If they weren't in public, he wouldn't have been able to control himself.

And yet, she seemed unaffected. She settled back in his arms and chatted with the other couples about their experiences at the resort, asking what they'd tried so far, which restaurants they liked the best, and more.

When their tour guide came and got them loaded onto the boat, he relinquished his hold on Jennie momentarily, but pulled her down on the bench seat next to him in the boat.

He let one hand trail up and down her velvety back as Jennie started to work the tour guide for information. Somehow, she struck up a conversation about wanting to work as a tour guide in a marina just like this.

The next thing Chad knew, she's getting information about busy seasons and slow seasons, how many trips the marina did in a day, and what the tour guides were paid.

It never ceased to amaze Chad. People would turn over their bank statements to Jennie if she asked them to. The guy didn't look the least bit fazed by her questions and she'd somehow managed to draw the other couples into the conversation as though it were completely natural.

He should be contributing in some way, but there really wasn't a damned thing he could add. So, he sat back and watched the way the sun glinted off her strawberry curls. He watched the way her eyes sparkled when she laughed and the way she leaned toward whoever was talking and looked at them as though they really mattered to her.

That's why she was so good at this. People wanted to connect with her. They were drawn to her. Chad was an expert on the topic of being drawn to Jennie.

He'd been drawn to her since the first time he'd spotted her at Sutton Capital. He had gone to ask Jack a question. He was having a bad day and was hurried and stressed, but he turned the corner and spotted Jennie at the desk outside Jack's office and froze. And, then she looked up at him and smiled. That smile cut right to his heart every time she graced him with it.

The attraction only grew from there. When Jack married Kelly and they all started hanging out outside the office together, he got his first glimpse of Jennie laughing. She always tipped her head back and laughed with such abandon. He found himself trying to make her laugh over and over again.

Sitting on the boat with his hands on her bare skin, Chad knew he would regret the closeness later when reality came racing back to him. But, he couldn't stop himself.

He'd let himself pretend, for the next few hours, that Jennie was his. That they had a life together, a future together. That this scenario wasn't some masquerade to get information for Jack's friend.

Yeah. It would suck when he came falling back to earth, but for right now, he would let himself fly high on the fantasy of Jennie.

CHAPTER 14

*T*hat evening, they were drinking beer out on the patio, sharing the double chaise lounge. The sexual tension that always whirled around them was present, but they were both getting better at living with it, or so it seemed to Jennie.

She suspected it wouldn't ever go away but they were building more of a friendship than they ever had on other assignments. And, they were definitely getting good at forgetting they were supposed to have a professional, working relationship.

Chad opened a new beer and handed the icy cold bottle to Jennie.

"Truth or dare?" she asked. They'd been playing for a while now, each of them repeatedly choosing 'truths' and skipping the 'dares.' It was as if they'd both forgotten they worked together. That Chad was her boss. That they shouldn't interact like this.

"Truth," he answered.

"Most unusual place you've ever had sex."

He shook his head with a laugh, but answered anyway. "Top of a mountain. We were hiking and we got to the top of a very isolated peak. We were hidden on one side by a boulder but anyone on the mountain peak across from us would have seen what was going on. They couldn't see detail, but, uh," he cleared his throat, "the general gist of it would have been clear."

Jennie didn't say anything in response. She was too busy picturing sex on top of a mountain with Chad. Would it be fast and dirty or would he take his time despite the fact that anyone could spot them at any time?

She was amazed at how quickly the images in her head had her breasts feeling heavier and the heat and anticipation of arousal swirling in her belly. She had to fight to draw her focus back to the game.

"Truth or dare?" Chad asked.

"Truth."

"What's your biggest fear?"

She opened her mouth to answer, but he quickly amended his question.

"Besides fish," he said with a grin.

Forgetting my husband? Falling in love again? Losing my entire life, my reason for being—again?

"Pass," Jennie said, invoking her one pass they'd negotiated for at the start of their game.

She continued before Chad had a chance to comment. "Truth or dare, Chad?"

"Truth," he said, raising his beer bottle to his lips again. Her eyes fell to his mouth involuntarily, before she ripped them away.

"What's your biggest fear?" She asked.

Chad turned to face her, answering without hesitation. "That I'll turn out like my father."

Chad's father had left his mother when he was in his early twenties, after twenty-five years of what everyone thought was a perfect marriage. He didn't cheat on her, didn't leave because he fell in love with someone else.

He simply left one day and didn't even bother to seek anything in the divorce. Kelly had told Jennie once that the last anyone heard of him, he was living on a beach in New Zealand or something.

Jennie started laughing, drawing a look from Chad that might have scared any other woman. Or, at least sobered them enough to stop laughing. For Jennie, it only made her laugh harder.

"I tell you my greatest fear and you're laughing at me?" He seemed truly offended as she shook her head at him, trying to catch her breath so she could explain.

"I'm laughing because it's not even remotely possible." She wiped at tears under her eyes. "It's so far from possible it's...well, it's just laughable. There isn't anything in you that would let you walk away from your family like that, Chad. I don't know what happened to your dad, but it's not in you to do that. When you love, when you commit, you'll do it forever."

Jennie sobered as she finished, realizing he would give his heart to someone one day. And it wouldn't be her.

That thought hit her harder than she'd thought it would. She didn't want him to give his heart to someone else, but she also couldn't face the idea of letting him give it to her.

Letting him love her with all his heart and soul, the way she knew he'd love. She turned to face the ocean as Chad seemed to process what she said. After several minutes, he quietly resumed the game.

"Truth or dare, Jen?"

"Truth," Jennie said. When Chad didn't respond right away, she turned to look at him through her lashes and found him watching her.

"Truth," she said again.

"Why did you back off that time we kissed? Was it because of your husband?" His voice was quiet now.

His question made Jennie freeze, her beer halfway to her mouth. She knew exactly what he was asking about. She'd kissed him once. And, for a minute, she forgot about Kyle. For one glorious, wonderful, breathtaking minute. One gut-wrenching, tortuous, heartbreaking minute she'd forgotten the man she loved.

The realization that Chad could make her forget her husband both broke her heart and scared the hell out of her at the same time. She lowered her beer and kept her eyes on the ocean. "I didn't know you knew about...about Kyle."

Chad's eyes were gentle but they bore into her the same as they always did. "Background check. I always run them when someone joins Sutton. I never said anything because it wasn't really related to the job. And, you never talked about him so I figured you didn't want anyone to know."

"Yeah, that makes sense. I guess I never thought about that."

And then she recited the facts about her and Kyle's marriage and his death. She recited them as if they were nothing more than facts.

Not as if they were the fundamental pieces of her life that had been torn apart, never to be put back together again. It was the only way she could get through it.

Chad was quiet while she told her story, and for several minutes afterward, and she was glad. Most people gasped and told her how sorry they were. Which did nothing to help her.

There was nothing that could fix her pain and Chad seemed to know this. After a minute, he took her hand and laced his fingers in hers, but still he didn't speak.

"I pulled away the day we kissed because I...I don't know. I just can't even imagine being with anyone other than Kyle, you know?" She didn't expect an answer and he didn't give one. She knew that Chad did get it. Somehow, he understood.

She raised her bottle to her mouth and took a sip. "Truth or dare?" she asked.

A long drawn out moment passed before Chad answered. "Truth."

"What are you thinking right now?"

Chad cleared his throat. "That you're strong as hell. That I

hate that there's nothing I can say or do to take away your pain."
He paused. "That I want to go back to easier questions."

She laughed but there wasn't much humor in it.

"Truth or dare?" Chad asked.

"Truth."

They played on, well into the night, keeping the topics light
and fun from then on. As with everything between the two of
them, it eventually snaked back around to sex and Chad threw
back a question Jennie had asked him earlier.

"Kinkiest thing you've ever done." Chad's answer had made
Jennie blush when she asked the question earlier in the night.

She squirmed, not wanting to tell Chad, but, he'd know if she
lied. He always did.

She focused on the corner of the label on her beer bottle,
peeling it away from the sweaty glass so she wouldn't have to
meet his eyes.

"When we were in college, Kyle bought me these panties that,
um..." she started. "They had, um, well, they were battery operated. And he had the remote control. We'd be studying and he
could turn them on whenever he wanted and I couldn't stop him.
He'd get all turned on knowing he was teasing the crap out of me
and, well, clearly I'd get all worked up. We'd see who could hold
out the longest without jumping the other one."

She thought back and laughed. "I don't think it was really fair,
though."

"Wh..." Chad cleared his throat. "Why not?"

"When he lost, it just meant he had to do the dishes. When I
lost, I got a spanking." She was laughing but as soon as she said it
she remembered how hot it had been when Kyle won.

She looked up at Chad and realized she'd probably had way
too much to drink. That wasn't a story she should have told. He
was looking down at her, eyes intense and heated and focused
only on her. She swallowed.

Chad got up suddenly and put his beer on the table next to

them. He walked in the house without saying a word. Jennie followed, laughing.

"Where are you going?"

He didn't answer.

"Chad?" Jennie padded after him, a little wobbly on her feet after so many beers.

He walked in the bathroom but didn't shut the door. He walked straight to the shower, stepped in with his clothes on, head down, as he turned the water on full blast.

She burst out laughing at the sight of him.

"Oh my God! Chad, what are you doing?"

He kept his back to her. "Taking a cold shower, Jen."

"You're crazy!"

He raised one hand to wave her off as he continued to let the water stream down over him.

"Nite, Jen. Get some sleep."

CHAPTER 15

*C*had woke with a headache. The cold shower had done little to erase the effects of Jennie's vibrating panties confession. His dreams had been filled with images of her moaning and squirming underneath his hands.

He knew they'd played with fire last night and he paid the price for it all night long as he chased her from dream to dream. From fantasy to fantasy.

It didn't help that they'd had too much to drink either. It started with margaritas at dinner and ended with beer at the villa. Way too much beer. And too much talking.

Chad would've liked to focus on Jennie's story about her very special little panties this morning, but his head was stuck on the fact that she was nowhere near over her husband. He suspected as much, but knowing it for sure seemed to cut deeper somehow. There were no words for how he felt about that.

Maybe his mom was right. Maybe he did do this to himself on purpose.

Well, if he did, he was damn good at it. What better woman to pick, if he subconsciously didn't want things to work out, than a woman who was not only off limits because of their work roles, but who was also in love with her dead husband?

How do you compete with a ghost? A perfect ghost who was her soul mate in every way even when they were growing up?

Shoot me now.

Chad heard a groan come from the bedroom and knew Jennie was struggling as much as he was this morning. He sat up slowly and swung his legs to the floor. Sleeping on the couch was killing his back and his neck. He stretched out and stood to try and work out the kinks, then reached for the phone.

Jennie came out just as he hung up.

"Hey," he said. "I ordered room service. Thought we'd stay in and try to recover this morning."

She smiled at him but her eyes were tired and sad. He figured she could've done without the recap of her life with Kyle last night.

"Thanks. I don't know if I can eat. I haven't had that much to drink in years," she said, rubbing her stomach. She got quiet for a minute and studied her feet. "Can I ask you a favor, Chad?"

"Anything. You know that." He didn't like how vulnerable she looked.

"Only Kelly knows about...about what I told you last night. Can you, um, not tell anyone else?"

Aw hell. He hated seeing her hurting. He wanted to fix everything for her. Hell, he'd bring back Kyle for her if he could, even if that meant seeing her with another man.

"Of course, Jennie. I promise." He paused, then grinned at her, knowing he needed to take the edge off and make her smile. "I won't tell anyone about your vibrating panties."

"Gah! You...you..." She threw a flip flop at him and stomped off to the shower. But at least she was laughing. That's all Chad could hope for now.

CHAPTER 16

They were almost at the end of their two weeks. Just four more nights. Kelly had called the day before and, so far, her doctor wasn't predicting delivery any time soon. Even though Jack had said he had a jet standing by for them, Jennie still worried about Kelly delivering the baby before they got home.

She and Chad had become closer than ever, which was nice in some ways, but it did make resisting the pull of their sexual attraction a lot harder. They'd only held hands or danced a bit in public to keep up the pretense of being a happily married couple. But, even that little bit of closeness had Jennie tense and uneasy. Her body cried out for Chad with everything in it and she felt more than physical attraction at this point, but her heart also ached with every pull.

And Jennie was utterly exhausted from trying to fight it. She sat on the edge of the bed while Chad showered. And she did something she hadn't done in a long time. She talked to Kyle. Not out loud. Only in her head. She needed him to know.

Please, Kyle. Please forgive me for this. I just want one night to forget. One night to not feel like I've been torn in half. To not remember. Just one night.

She took a deep breath and looked at the door to the bathroom and stood, pulling off her robe and letting it drop to the floor. She pushed open the door and stepped into the steamy room.

She knew Chad heard her. His back tensed right away and his hands stilled. He lowered his head and waited, and she wondered what thoughts would go through his head.

She slipped into the shower in front of him, turning as she did so she could see his face. He watched her so warily, holding his hands still. Not touching her or reaching for her.

She placed her palms flat on his chest and felt the sharp inhale of his breath. She looked up at him, thankful for the water that streamed over them. She didn't want him to see her tears as she let her hands slip over the slick warmth of his skin.

"Make me forget, Chad. For one night. Please? Make me forget."

He looked down at her, eyes blazing with heat, but also sadness. She didn't want him to be sad for her and she didn't want to make him sad. But, she couldn't walk away anymore. She just couldn't fight what was happening between them any longer.

As Chad looked down at Jennie, he knew he should walk away. Say no and leave it alone. But he couldn't do that. He'd lost all his strength to fight this attraction and he didn't want to walk away. He didn't want to fight it.

He wanted her so badly, all he could think about was what she would taste like. What she would feel like, her soft body against his. The way she would feel when she wrapped her legs around him.

The way he could make her feel, make her squirm and cry out for him. What it would feel like to bury himself, to sink into the wet heat of her body and lose himself in the way she felt.

His mind had been scrambled since they got on the plane for Florida and it had taken everything he had in him to fight it the last ten days. With her here, asking him to touch her, he didn't want to try to fight this anymore.

If he only got this one night, then so be it. He'd take one night if that's all she could give him.

"Are you sure, Jennie? We can't take this back if we do this."

She nodded.

He leaned down and trapped her, arms on either side of her against the wall of the shower as his heart pounded in his chest. He was so close to what he'd wanted for so long, but he had to be sure she truly wanted this.

"Say it. Tell me you want this," he said softly. Urgently. He could hear the need in his own voice and he could see a matching need in her eyes.

"I want this, Chad. For one night, I want this." Her voice didn't falter or waiver.

It was like unleashing a force he could no longer control. He leaned in and kissed her sweet, succulent mouth as he pressed her against the wall of the shower with his body and took what he had needed for so long.

He knew he shouldn't. It was the most selfish, heartless thing he'd ever done, but he was defenseless against Jennie's power.

He ignored the fact that she still loved her husband, that she hadn't healed from the wounds his death had left and he took her.

Chad swept his tongue inside her mouth in a forceful, needy move. She met him with as much heat and desire and passion.

He lifted her, holding her on one of his thighs as he moved his mouth to her neck. He brushed his lips across her soft skin, taking in the sweet, silky feel of her. Breathing in that scent that was innately Jennie.

One hand closed on her breast as his mouth moved to capture the other one, covering her nipple. Jennie held the back of his head tight, pressing him to her as she arched her back and moaned. The sound hit him hard, going right to his already rock-hard cock.

Her nipples pebbled for him as he let his tongue swirl around them, grazing them with his teeth from time to time as she writhed in his arms. He'd never in his life experienced anything like the feel of Jennie in his arms.

All of his fantasies about her—and they had been plentiful and detailed and dirty—were nowhere close to the reality of her and the way she responded to his touch.

Chad slipped his hand between her legs and felt how wet she was already. He couldn't stop himself. He lifted her higher and positioned himself between her legs.

She sank down so slowly on him, he thought he would burst. Or beg for mercy. The feeling of being inside Jennie was like nothing he ever could have imagined. She gripped him tightly and rocked her hips back and forth, tearing an almost animal-like sound from his lips.

He sank into her deep and hard, long slow strokes that made him ache for more. He never wanted this to end.

It took everything he had to stop them. Chad lifted Jennie off his cock and put her on the floor, reaching over to turn off the water.

"Condom," he whispered as his mouth found hers again. "Bed."

He skipped the towel and lifted her into his arms. He wanted back inside her. Now.

But when he got her to the bed and dug in his wallet for a condom, he placed it on the nightstand. She needed more than this. She needed to forget and he damn well was going to give her that.

Chad lowered himself to her peaches and cream thighs and let his hands travel over her heated flesh. Everything about her was softness to his hardness. He marveled at the feel of her; at how incredible she looked spread out for him.

For a minute, he thought of all the things he would do to her someday, but he made himself push those thoughts from his mind. There would be no someday between them. He knew better than to hope for more than this one night with her.

In fact, Chad was pretty confident it wouldn't even be one full night. As soon as she remembered Kyle, she'd be done. He had this moment. Nothing more.

Driving everything else from his mind, Chad trailed his tongue slowly over Jennie's flush skin, the swollen nub that would bring her pleasure and help her lose herself. He almost groaned out loud at the sweet taste of her.

He closed his mouth over her clitoris and tugged gently as she pushed her hips up, seeking more. She was swollen and wet and responding instantly to every touch, every movement.

He slipped one, then two fingers inside of her, wanting to hear the sweet little moans she made as she quivered in his hands. Holding her hips still with one hand, he circled and licked, then sucked hard once again. Her orgasm ripped through her in waves, muscles pulsing and throbbing from her release.

She came fast and hard and Chad knew she needed a lot more. His hands roamed her body, stopping to play with the soft rounds of her breasts. He kissed the soft plane of her stomach, luxuriating in the feel of her as he waited for her to come down from her orgasm. Then, just as quickly, he let his fingers and his mouth settle on her as he sent her spiraling up again.

Her muscles clamped down on his fingers as she crested the wave of her second orgasm and Chad's body screamed to be inside her. To know what it felt like to have her come around him as her moans and whimpers filled his ears.

Chad slowly withdrew his fingers and kissed his way back up Jennie's body, finding her mouth once more. He didn't let her rest. He didn't want her thinking or remembering.

He tore open the condom and rolled it on as she reached with greedy hands for his hard length. The touch of her hands was almost enough to do him in. He pinned her wrists above her head with one hand and lowered himself over her.

He entered her, intending to move slowly, to draw out the pleasure, both for her and for himself. But his tiny vixen wrapped her legs around him and pulled.

He laughed and let her pull him deep inside, letting out a groan when he'd buried himself deep and hard.

Jennie buried her head in his neck and he plunged into her hot, wet depths, greedily taking everything she had to give. He gritted his teeth, resisting the almost overwhelming urge to let himself go.

He leaned down and worshipped her neck, licking and biting at the soft spot behind her ear until he heard her moan. He worked his way down her neck and across her shoulder as he plunged ever deeper into her in steady strokes that took them both closer to orgasm with each one.

The feel of her around him was more than he could ever have imagined, though he had tried time and time again. He'd fantasized about this moment almost every day.

He'd give everything to have more than this one night with her. To make love to her slowly one night, then bracingly hard and fast the next. To make love while they laughed and played and experimented.

To have her over him, looking down with her sweet, sensuous eyes as she rode him to ecstasy. To take her from behind or up against a wall. He wanted Jennie again and again in every way imaginable.

When his mouth reached her breast, he bit down gently, tugging with his teeth as Jennie cried out. He felt her clenching muscles grip him and knew there was no fighting it. Chad gave in and buried himself with a deep guttural growl as he came inside her for what he knew would be the first and last time.

Pleasure poured through him as he emptied himself. He gave

himself a minute to lay still inside of her, satiated and spent. He told himself time and time again not to wish for more. Not to hope that she might come out of this changed somehow, and able to love him.

Able to move on from her love for a man who was no longer with her, but still somehow between them as though he were a tangible presence.

He shook off foolish dreams and slipped out of the bed and cleaned up in the bathroom. When he returned, Jennie was facing away from him and he guessed she couldn't handle looking at him or talking to him right now. That was okay. They could talk in the morning.

He slid into the bed with her and wrapped an arm around her, pulling her tight. He wouldn't let her sleep alone tonight. For this one night, he'd hold her tight and wrap her up in his arms. And, maybe, just maybe she'd forget for a little while longer.

She turned toward him, snuggling into his shoulder for a long time. She opened her doe eyes and looked up at him, tearing his heart in two with the trust she held in those eyes for him, and the objection she could see coming to the surface.

"One night," he whispered, and dropped a kiss to her lips.

He felt her nod. Then he heard her take a deep breath and she sank into his arms to sleep.

CHAPTER 17

*W*hen Jennie woke, the other side of her bed was empty. She knew he'd probably gone for a run on the beach and she was glad to have the time to herself.

She didn't regret last night, but she did hope it didn't destroy the friendship they had. She wanted Chad in her life.

Her mind flashed back to the sight of Chad standing above her, heat burning in his eyes, need evident in every sculpted muscle of his body. She remembered the feel of his mouth and hands on her body.

Chad brought her body to places she had never dreamed of going. And, she couldn't fight him. She couldn't fight the pull he seemed to have on her.

She'd been in ecstasy last night when he took her from one orgasm to the next with ease. The feel of his hard, strong body over her, inside her, taking her over completely. It was primal and raw, and even the memory was enough to make her ache with need again.

But her body now warred with her heart and her mind and the memories of her husband. Jennie was still in love with a man who could never hold her again, never make love to again.

There wasn't room in her heart for Chad when Kyle still held such a big place there. She'd had her one night with Chad. She needed to put him out of her mind now.

In a near daze, she pulled on her clothes and went out the sliding glass doors to the small patio off the bedroom. She sat in one of the chairs and pulled her knees to her chest, resting her head on her knees.

As she sat, she let memories of another trip to the beach wash over her. She and Kyle had been young when they married, so a trip to a tropical getaway like this hadn't been possible. But their families rented them a little house in Hilton Head for the week. The road trip down had been one of the happiest times Jennie could remember.

At the time, she'd thought they had so much ahead of them. A whole lifetime. A lifetime that turned out to be not very long at all.

They were so carefree then. Before the doctors and the hospitals and the fear. Before the knowledge that Kyle wasn't going to make it. That there'd be no miracle for him—for them.

She never told any of her friends how hard she and Kyle had tried to get pregnant after the diagnosis. She worried that people would think she was sick and twisted for wanting to have her dying husband's baby. But, she didn't care.

She'd wanted to have his baby so badly. But they hadn't been lucky enough. His sperm had been frozen before his treatment, but when he didn't survive, she'd been hurting too much to think of having a child without him by her side.

Jennie looked out onto the beach and remembered the sand castle she and Kyle had built on their honeymoon. They'd built bedrooms in their castle.

One for them and three others, one for each of the children they'd hoped to have someday. They were so young and hopeful then. So completely naive and clueless about what lay in store for them.

It had been so easy to believe they had a long life together ahead of them. So easy to believe nothing could touch them.

~

Chad stopped when he spotted Jennie on the patio. She hadn't seen him yet so he watched her quietly. He knew instantly that he'd made a big mistake. A selfish, heartless mistake that Jennie was now paying for.

She might have said she wanted that to happen last night, but he could see the anguish and sadness that surrounded her right now. It was palpable, a creature in its own right.

Chad cursed and knew he had to make sure she understood he would never push for them to be together as lovers again. He wouldn't put her through that even once more. He slowly walked toward her chair. As he approached the villa, the phone rang and he saw Jennie slip inside to answer it. He picked up his pace and jogged the last yards.

Jennie looked up when she saw him come in.

"Hey, Jack," she said into the phone. "Chad just came in. Let me put you on speaker."

"Morning Jack," Chad said as he grabbed a bottle of water and sat on the couch opposite Jennie.

"Hey, guys. Kelly says hi and she's not showing any signs of going into labor yet, so enjoy your last few days," Jack said.

Jennie looked up and smiled at Chad, but there was a tentativeness to it, as though she wasn't sure she should be happy about having a few more days.

His heart skipped a beat. He needed to find a way to forget the most amazing night of his life, but he hoped her smile meant that they would still be able to be friends after last night. That things wouldn't be weird between them.

Hell, who was he kidding? Things would be weird. He just hoped they hadn't completely killed their friendship.

"So, what have you got? Anything interesting there?" Jack asked.

Her eyes snapped to Chad's and he knew she was thinking the same thing he was.

She was thinking about how interesting things had gotten between them last night.

Chad shook his head, clearing his thoughts and focusing on the call with Jack. Last night with Jennie had been one night. Just like she'd asked for. He had to move on now.

Chad set down his water bottle. "Not really. The resort is busy and the service and rooms are first class. The restaurants have been good. It seems like business is strong. I can definitely say the nephews don't seem to do much to earn their keep. It appears the managers are running the show. We've seen the nephews partying and schmoozing, but that's all they seem to do. They're kind of what you'd expect on a Girls Gone Wild video, but a little more subdued, given the high-class nature of the resort."

"I had a feeling. I wonder what their uncle plans to do with them after he sells the resort. It'll give Peter an immediate savings in expenses, though. He'll be happy to hear that. What about the marina? That whole thing still seems odd to me. Were you able to spot any reason for setting things up the way they have?" Jack asked.

"No," Chad said. "They definitely only have that setup for the marina, though. The other tours are all set up traditionally, with the reps working the lobby and running their own billing. More along the lines of what I've seen at other places."

"We've looked into ownership of the company running the marina and it's owned by a company called Florifish, Inc. It's a privately held company but, here's the thing. It's owned primarily by the Masters brothers and a guy named Rick Bandon. Bandon is a building inspector in Florida," Jack explained. "There are a few other small shareholders as well, but those three are the main players."

"I wonder if Jonathan Masters knows his nephews are owners in a company that seems to be taking advantage of his resort. The contract Florifish has with the resort hardly seems equitable. The resort is doing all the work for very little return," Chad said.

"There are also tax implications for all that money the resort is running through there. It doesn't make any sense from a business standpoint to take on the workload and tax burden for such a small cut. It's a lot of work. They're booking five fishing boats a day, seven scuba tours on the smaller boats. That's a lot of work when they could turn the work over to the marina company and charge a flat rate for the lease or even a sliding scale lease based on sales and use," Jack said.

Chad knew he was mostly talking to himself now, mulling over the scenarios in his head.

"Three fishing boats," Jennie said.

"What?" Chad and Jack asked as one.

Jennie leaned toward the phone. "Three fishing boats, five of the smaller boats they use for the scuba and sightseeing tours, twenty-seven kayaks."

Jack was quiet for a minute but they could hear papers shuffling.

"No. They have bills showing five fishing boats, seven rigid inflatables going out on dive tours three times a day, and forty-five kayaks," Jack said.

Jennie was shaking her head even though Jack couldn't see her through the phone. "That's not what they have. Unless maybe they have boats at another spot? Maybe some of the tours leave from somewhere else?"

"We never thought to ask that," Chad said.

Jennie stood. "I'll go ask one of my friends at the desk."

"I want to get Andrew in on this. Chad, stay by the phone. I'll call you back. Jennie, see what you can find out. If they're billing for stuff that doesn't exist, I want to know about it." Jack cut the connection as Jennie looked under the couch and around the floor for her sandals.

Chad crossed to the front door and picked them up. He handed them to her with a wry smile. They were always right where he put them, but Jennie still hadn't figured out to look for them there.

"Oh! Thanks." She grinned then slid her feet into the shoes and opened the door. "Be right back," she called over her shoulder.

Chad sank onto the couch and waited for Jack to call them back as he thought about the night before. Other than a few uneasy looks here and there, she was acting as if everything was normal. God, he hoped she was okay with last night.

In a way, he wanted to regret it. He wanted to feel like he'd done something wrong, and on the one hand he did, but a part of him couldn't be sorry for what happened.

Having the chance to hold Jennie in his arms for one night had been incredible. He didn't know if she could ever give him more than that, but he'd take what he could. He'd take the memory of one night with her if that's all he could have.

The phone rang, pulling him out of his thoughts. Chad picked it up, knowing it would be either Jack or Andrew.

"Yeah, guys," he said.

"Chad, I want you guys out of there. The jet's on standby. Get to the airstrip and get out of there now," Jack said, the urgency in his tone sending cold disquiet through Chad.

"They're laundering money," Andrew explained. "That's the only reason to run that money through there like that and the only explanation for billing for boats that don't exist. And, whoever the hell those idiot nephews have gotten into bed with won't be nice people. Nice people don't need to clean their money. My guess is the building inspector, Bandon, they've partnered up with is taking bribes."

Chad was already up, grabbing his backpack and Jennie's

purse then heading for the door. If they had time to get back and pack their stuff, they would.

But, he wanted to be ready in case Jennie's questions raised red flags. If the shit hit the fan, then at least they had what they needed. They'd replace the clothes and other things later.

"I'm going. I'll call you when we're on the plane." He didn't wait for them to answer. He needed to get to Jennie.

Since she'd never suspect anything like this, she might ask one too many questions. Their undercover work was never dangerous. It had always been almost a joke to call it undercover.

He suddenly realized the position he'd put her in, the danger she could be in right now. It was always possible someone would resent the way she brought information to light on a job. She could be on the receiving end of retribution or a vendetta at any time.

Never mind the way he'd just walked her right straight into a situation with people who were very likely quite dangerous. He felt as if someone had sliced him open and gutted him. If anything happened to Jennie, he would never forgive himself.

Chad jogged along the secluded path and up to the main building of the resort with only one thing on his mind. Jennie. Getting to her and getting her to safety.

CHAPTER 18

*J*ennie crossed the lobby to the front desk, glad to see her friend Tracy was working there. She'd spent many days chatting with Tracy and pulling bits and pieces of information from her. She genuinely liked the woman. She seemed to work hard and actually care about the experience the guests at the resort had.

Jennie slipped into airhead mode.

"Hi, Tracy!"

"Hi, Jennie. How are you today?" Tracy asked, her smile wide.

Jennie pouted in an overly dramatic way that would have had her cringing if she'd seen it on another woman. The staff here was trained to cater to those pouts instead of cringe. "We only have three days left here and Chad mentioned wanting to go out on a fishing boat. It always seems like all the boats are out. Are they all booked?"

Her friend's face fell. "I'm sorry. I'm afraid they are. The fishing trips book several weeks in advance. In fact, most people book them when they book their reservations for the resort. Apparently, sitting and waiting for a fish to bite a hook is quite popular," Tracy said, wry humor in her voice.

"Oh no. I really wanted to take Chad fishing. You guys don't have other boats you could bring in or another location we could take a trip from?"

If Tracy thought the questions were odd, she didn't show it. She just shook her head. "I'm afraid not. We only have the three boats and they fill up fast. Our dock isn't big enough for more than that."

Jennie feigned disappointment and said good-bye. As she walked away from the front desk, she headed toward the staircase that would bring her out to the hallways leading to some of the rooms.

She'd seen a doorway marked private right before the stairs and wondered if there were offices back there. Maybe even the nephews' offices.

With a quick peek over her shoulder to ensure that Tracy was distracted by one of the other guests, Jennie slipped through the door and walked down the hall of the private area.

There were offices on each side of the hallway, but they were all quiet and empty. Except for the office at the end. Jennie heard voices coming from that one and she recognized the speakers immediately. The Masters brothers.

She walked quietly down the carpeted hall 'till she stood close enough to hear the conversation. She didn't know the voices well enough to tell right off which one was Matt Masters and which one was Alan Masters, so she listened as the conversation developed.

"Shit! There has to be ten thousand in here this time," one voice said.

"So wh-wh-what?" came the reply. That must be Alan.

He had a stutter that was so mild most of the time, it was barely noticeable, but something was making it more pronounced now. Nerves, maybe?

"We can't keep running these large amounts through here. Someone will notice if we don't stick to smaller numbers," said the other voice, which Jennie now surmised must be Matt.

"We have to run through whatever Rick tells us to. He w-won't let us stop now," said Alan.

"He has to let us stop. We didn't agree to this much. And, I'll tell you one thing, brother. There's no way all of this is for him anymore. No way he's taking in ten thou a week. I'm telling you, he's got us cleaning money for other people now. If we're gonna take that kind of risk, I want a bigger cut."

Jennie bit her cheeks to keep from gasping and backpedaled down the hallway. She and Chad had gotten into something a lot more dangerous than they were used to.

Well, at least than she was used to. Chad dealt with this kind of thing all the time when he was in the military, but she sure as hell didn't have this kind of experience.

Jennie's breathing suddenly sounded too loud in her ears—as if it would fill the hallway and alert the brothers to her presence any minute now.

In her rush to get away from a conversation she shouldn't be listening to, she tripped over a decorative table, knocking over the vase of flowers that sat at its center. The clunk of the thick glass hitting the hard wood seemed to echo around her.

"What was that?" she heard from the room down the hall.

She panicked, looking around her frantically, for a way to get away. A place to hide. She was too far from the door that led to the lobby to make it down the hallway safely. She ducked into another open doorway. An office.

There was nowhere to hide in the room she'd entered. The desk was open at the bottom on both sides, so she couldn't crouch down there. The door opened out into the hallway so there was no way hide behind it. She was trapped.

Jennie looked down and saw her hands were shaking. She focused on slowing her breathing, listening for any sound from the hallway. She didn't have her cell phone with her and she couldn't remember Chad's number to use the office phone on the desk to call him.

The hallway was quiet and still for a minute but then the tell-tale cadence of shoes sounded on the tile floor. Jennie knew they'd find her any second.

With a small curse, she pulled off her favorite sandals. She quickly snapped the heel off one of them. In reality, they only had a one-and-a-half-inch heel so a heel would be unlikely to snap as she was walking in them, but she was banking on the brothers not knowing that.

She braced herself with one hand on the wall in the small office and waited.

"Oh, help. Can you guys help me?" She took a couple of little hopping steps toward them. Not the direction she really wanted to go, but at this point, she needed to go toward them before she could get away from them.

"What are you doing back here? This area is off limits," barked Alan.

"It is?" Jennie batted her eyelashes. "I'm sorry. I twisted my ankle and I thought the infirmary was back here. Can you guys help me?" She held up the broken sandal as evidence of her plight and held her breath.

The men walked toward her slowly and she couldn't tell if they were buying her story or not. Nerves settled firmly in her stomach as she began to wish she hadn't tried to dig so deep for information this time.

She'd give anything to be back at the villa with Chad right now. She watched the two men approach and remembered how empty and abandoned this hallway was.

They're not buying this.

Alan reached out and grabbed her arm. Hard.

Jennie swallowed and her voice sounded small, almost foreign to her ears. "I'm looking for the infirmary. My ankle—"

"Calm down, Alan," Matt said, placing a hand on his brother's arm.

Alan dropped Jennie's arm, but before she could try to get

away, Matt had an arm around her shoulder. He was being gentler than his brother, but there was no mistaking the firm pressure guiding her back down the hall toward their office.

"We'll help you in our office," he said.

Her mind was scrambled as she ran through possible ways to get out of this. Should she scream and run down the hall? If she did that, they'd definitely know she overheard them.

If she didn't make it to the lobby in time, she'd be trapped. And, she wasn't completely sure any of the employees would be willing to risk their jobs and take on the brothers even if she did get their attention.

Should she go with them to their office and hope she could talk her way out of this? She was a master at playing dumb, but the thought of going even further away from the populated spots on the resort with these guys made her feel sick.

Unfortunately, she didn't think she had a choice. She took a deep breath and started to let Matt walk her toward his office. A tight knot of nerves settled in the pit of her stomach.

She was in trouble.

CHAPTER 19

*C*had made himself slow to a walk when he entered the lobby. Jennie had a habit of poking and prodding for answers. If she asked the wrong question here, she might put herself in danger, but he didn't want to let on that anything was wrong.

He scanned the front desk, but she wasn't there. One of the women he'd seen Jennie chat up a number of times stood behind the desk.

He approached and nodded a greeting to the woman, putting on his meathead facade. "Hey," he grunted. "You seen Jennie?"

"Oh, you just missed her! She was here, but she went out the east stairwell. If you hurry, you might catch her." The woman gestured to the stairwell with a smile and Chad nodded.

He pulled some cash from his pocket put it on the counter. Hopefully, it was enough.

"We're heading out with some friends to spend the last few days on a boat. I need our bags and a car out front right away." Chad knew most people did what they were told when he gave them an order.

He didn't wait for an answer. He headed toward the east stairwell. When he spotted the door marked 'Private' before he reached the stairs, he knew exactly where Jennie had gone.

Chad stopped by the door and pulled his cell phone out, acting as if he were going to call his wife. Through lowered lids, he watched until the woman at the front desk turned away, and then slipped through the doorway.

When he turned, his heart dropped into his stomach. Jennie was being led down the hall by the two idiot nephews and she didn't look like she wanted to be there. Chad broke into a jog again.

"There you are, baby," he said as he came up to her. "I'm starved. You know I gotta eat breakfast before ten or my stomach hurts. What are you doing back here?" He looked around, his meathead wrinkled brow firmly in place.

The nephews stopped their forward motion, but the one that had his arm around Jennie kept it there. She turned her sweet, trusting eyes to Chad and he could see the panic beneath her ditzy show.

"I hurt my ankle, baby. I fell." Jennie's eyes locked onto his, trusting and sure, as if she knew he'd get her out of this.

God, he loved this woman—even when she was playing dumb.

He scooped her up in his arms, easily extricating her from the man's grasp. "I've got you, babe. I'll take care of you." He dropped a kiss to her mouth and began to walk down the hall, carrying her away from the nephews.

These yahoos didn't worry him. It was the people they most likely worked for that had him sweating.

One of the nephews grabbed Chad's arm as he turned away and Chad felt Jennie tighten her hold on his neck.

"Hey, wait," the idiot nephew said.

Chad turned, looking down at the man's hand on his arm. "Yeah?" he grunted, staring down the smaller man. Chad knew most guys wouldn't argue with him when he turned up his scowl.

He waited a half beat but the guy didn't say anything. He dropped his arm and stepped back as Chad turned and left.

Chad didn't look back. He walked through the door to the lobby then set Jennie on her feet. They walked out the front door of the resort and Jennie slipped into one of the cabs waiting in the circular drive. He handed her a wad of cash.

If he spotted the brothers, he'd tell the driver to leave with Jennie and he'd catch up to her after dealing with Matt and Alan. Chad stood guard by the side of the cab while their luggage was loaded.

As he expected, the brothers didn't show. The luggage was loaded and Chad whisked Jennie away.

They didn't slow down until they reached the airstrip and boarded the small private jet Jack had waiting for them. And Chad didn't breathe easy again until Jennie was back in Connecticut, safely at home.

CHAPTER 20

*J*ennie walked down the hospital hallway, smiling absentmindedly at people she passed in the hall. Her stomach was flipping and churning. She knew when she arrived in Kelly's hospital room she'd likely see Chad for the first time in three days—she couldn't exactly avoid the situation.

Kelly had given birth to Madeleine Sophie Sutton three hours earlier. Jennie couldn't wait to hold such a tiny new life in her arms.

Even the nerves she felt at the prospect of seeing Chad for the first time since they returned from Florida wasn't scary enough to keep her away from her best friend today. It was just scary enough to keep her from being able to eat anything. Or take a deep breath. Or stop fidgeting.

She found the room and knocked on the door.

"Come in," came Kelly's voice from the other side.

Jennie pushed open the door and found Kelly sitting up in bed. She looked tired, but happier than Jennie had ever seen her. In her arms was a tiny pink creature with a scrunched-up face. She was ugly and beautiful, all at the same time.

And she was awake! Wide eyes looked around as Kelly beamed at Jennie.

"Oh, Kelly. She's beautiful," Jennie said as she sat on the edge of her friend's bed.

"I can't believe she's finally here. I never want to put her down." Kelly's smile was wide and almost glowing.

"Does that mean I don't get to hold her?" Jennie laughed. "I washed my hands and everything," she said, holding her hands up.

Kelly laughed and transferred Maddy into Jennie's arms. She was swaddled tightly in a striped blanket and she gazed up at Jennie. As Jennie watched, tired lids sank down over her eyes. Within minutes, the baby slept soundly in her arms.

"Wow. I think I could watch her forever." Jennie glanced up at Kelly before gazing back down at the baby.

She'd never seen anything like it. She was perfect in every way. Soft skin and fuzzy hair. A tiny button for a nose and little ears. Eyelashes that fluttered on her cheeks lightly as she slept.

"I know. They say newborns sleep for long stretches in the first one or two days. After that, we're supposedly in for feedings every two hours and nights without a lot of sleep. I'm trying to soak up the fun stuff right now before I become a walking zombie," Kelly said.

"Well, I'll come over and give you a break whenever you need it. You just call." She looked around the room for Jack. "Speaking of breaks, where is Jack?"

"He and Chad went out to get me some real food. The nurses said I can eat soon and Jack didn't want me to have to eat hospital food. I have to admit, I was a bit relieved. I'm starving after so many hours with nothing but ice chips and popsicles. And, hospital food doesn't exactly sound appealing."

The two women talked about babies and the size of tiny fingernails for another few minutes.

Jennie had suspected Kelly would bring up the Florida trip and she wasn't wrong.

"So, does Chad think you guys are in danger because of what

you found in Florida?" she asked. She had a strange look on her face that Jennie couldn't quite interpret.

"We're not sure what's going to happen yet. We met with Jonathan Masters to tell him what I overheard and it was awful, Kelly. The poor man was so shocked. I think he always knew his nephews were lazy but you could tell he had no idea they would do something like this. Then it hit him that they'd put his whole family at risk with this.

"The federal government will most likely seize the resort and if they try to go after the winery, the rest of the family could lose everything. His grandkids would lose their inheritance, all of it. Never mind the fact that the feds could decide to arrest Jonathan as well," Jennie said.

"I can't believe how selfish and stupid the nephews have been. You met them, right? What are they like?"

Jennie shook her head. "Arrogant and useless, for the most part. I can tell you one thing; I doubt they were the brains behind this. When you talk to Jonathan, it's hard to believe they're even related to him. He's the sweetest man. He totally understood when Jack told him we needed to report this. He wasn't angry at us at all. I think he was mostly just heartbroken over the whole thing."

Kelly picked at the blanket covering her in the hospital bed. "So, you and Chad will have to testify?"

Jennie nodded. "Most likely. And, mostly me. They might not need Chad at all since it was me who heard the brothers talking. But, Chad said federal investigations take a very long time. The FBI is notorious for investigations that last as many as five years, or even more. They tie everything up in a bow and won't go to trial until they have mountains of evidence ready to go.

"Jonathan Masters is getting his nephews a lawyer and they're going to try to convince the nephews to turn themselves in. Chad says at that point the feds will probably send the brothers back in to feed them evidence against the building inspector and whoever else is involved. The amount of money that was going through there couldn't be from a single inspector taking bribes. The FBI is going to want to know who they were laundering money for. They may end up not needing my testimony at all if the brothers start collecting evidence for them." Jennie looked up to see that strange look on Kelly's face again.

"Um, Jennie, I need to tell you—" Kelly started as the door opened and Chad and Jack walked back into the room.

"Hey, sweetheart, how are my girls?" asked Jack. He looked almost as worn out as Kelly but every bit as happy.

Jennie felt Chad's eyes on her and then the walls seemed to be closing in as if the room were filled with too many people.

Oh, who was she kidding?

It was Chad's presence that made the walls close in on her. Jennie suddenly felt like she'd never be able to take a deep breath again. She hated that her body responded so strongly to him— even more so, since their one night in Florida.

It was as if her body now knew what it could have and it wasn't willing to let go, even though Jennie ordered it to forget.

"I'm going to get going, guys. Kelly, I'll stop by tomorrow. They'll keep you here for two days, right? I can bring lunch tomorrow if you want," she said as she scooped up her purse and moved to the door.

She knew she was speaking just a little too quickly and she felt like everyone was staring at her, but she needed out of there. Now.

"Oh, you don't have to go. You just got here," Kelly said.

Jennie smiled and shook her head. "I'll be back. I'll come hold her while you nap tomorrow. Promise. I've got some errands to run now, though."

They said good-byes and Jennie slipped from the room, finally taking a deep breath as she started down the hall.

"Jen!" Chad called from behind her.

Damn.

She turned to find Chad coming toward her, hands shoved in his pockets. He looked more uneasy than she'd ever seen him.

"Hey," she said, smiling at him, but feeling like she couldn't breathe again.

He towered over her and she could see the concern in his eyes. "Are we okay, Jennie? Can we go back to the way things were between us? Before?"

He didn't have to clarify what he meant by 'before.' She knew perfectly well what he was asking about.

She nodded. She didn't trust herself to speak but he still watched her intently and she knew he wanted her confirmation. And, the truth was, Jennie didn't want to lose Chad.

Their time in Florida before 'that night' had brought them a lot closer than they used to be. They'd talked about so many things and spent more time with each other than she ever thought they would.

"We're good. It's okay, Chad," she said as she put on her brightest smile and ordered her nipples to stand down. "We really are okay, Chad, I promise."

He smiled. "Okay. See you at work then, Jen."

She turned and walked down the hall, hoping she was right. She didn't want to lose a friend she'd only begun to truly know.

Assistant United States Attorney, Caroline Waters, steered her sedan down the dirt driveway that served as the entrance to the abandoned building site. The location should have been an enormous mall by now, but the owner had run out of funds and the project was on hold. The lot was sufficiently isolated to serve Caroline's needs today.

She spotted Bandon waiting for her in his truck and pulled alongside him. She didn't plan to get out of the car for this talk. She hated coming to the filthy job sites he was used to.

In fact, she hated dealing with Bandon at all. She found him tactless and rude and he certainly didn't go to any lengths to hide the slimy, appreciative looks he gave her body whenever they met. It made her skin crawl, but he was a necessary evil at this point in her life.

When Caroline discovered just how hard it really was to pay off her law school debt on fifty thousand dollars a year, she decided there were two options. Go to work as a defense attorney instead of a prosecutor or pick and choose the crimes she really cared about prosecuting.

When she found a crime she didn't feel truly needed to be prosecuted, she offered the accused a chance to pay their way out of trouble. Then it was simply a matter of telling her boss the case they had wouldn't stick, there had been errors in the collection of evidence that would damage the case, or any number of other excuses. On a few occasions, she'd had to go a little further and arrange for evidence to disappear so no one would begin to see a pattern in her 'dropped' cases and suspect her.

All in all, she only needed to do it a few times a year to make the money she needed, and with any luck, she'd pay off her loans soon and be free of it all. And free of the likes of Rick Bandon.

For now, he was a necessary evil in laundering her funds for her. Things were getting to the point where she was going to need to buy shares in his marina company to keep everything looking above board, but with this recent complication, she was relieved her name wasn't on any of the books yet.

Bandon rolled down his window. "To what do I owe this unscheduled visit, Caroline? Not that I'm not always happy to get a call from you, but I hadn't expected to see you again until next month."

Caroline suppressed a shudder at the leer on Bandon's face. "We have a problem. The FBI has opened an investigation into Florifish. Those brothers you swore to me were so malleable and loyal are now feeding information to the FBI about your little endeavor."

"*My* little endeavor. You're in this as much as I am, lady. Don't you forget it." His words were big but she saw the swagger drain from Bandon's body as he slumped in his truck, absorbing the shock of the news.

"Luckily for you, I managed to get myself assigned to the case. They haven't brought in any information to implicate anyone other than you yet and I expect you to keep it that way," Caroline said.

"Well, where the hell will that leave me? Don't think I'll let you leave me hanging out to dry on this one, Ms. Big Wig Attorney. If I go down for this, I'll take you down, too," Bandon sneered.

Caroline held out a hand to stop him. She'd already thought this through. She knew perfectly well Bandon would turn against her if he were arrested for money laundering and she wouldn't be at all surprised to find out he had some kind of document or tape or something to hold over her head if push came to shove.

"I'll take care of the investigation, but you need to take care of those Masters brothers. They can't make their next meeting with their handler. There was, apparently, one other witness. I'll get her name and location for you as soon as I can. In the meantime, I suggest you keep that boat company running as a legitimate business and put all your other activities on hold for now. We need to do damage control."

Bandon stared at her for a few minutes.

She'd always suspected he was a sick bastard who wasn't afraid to get his hands dirty and she was right. As long as she laid out a plan, he'd pick it up and run with it. She was sure of it.

His voice was cold and unfeeling when he finally spoke. "Fine, I'll take care of the brothers. You get working on that other witness."

He gave only one curt nod before he drove away.

CHAPTER 21

For weeks, Chad and Jennie were a little stiff and awkward around one another, but it gradually began to go away. They fell back into the swing of things, with Jennie being a wise ass and Chad laughing at her like he used to.

Since he wasn't willing to lose her as a friend, it was the way things had to be. There wasn't any getting around it.

Thanks to Mrs. Poole, Jack and Kelly were back to hosting get-togethers at their house on a regular basis despite the fact they had a three-week-old baby. It made Chad laugh to think about it. He thought they would have taken a few months to get settled in, but they were hosting their first barbeque today.

Chad stepped out onto the porch and couldn't hold back his smile. His tough cousin, a man who ran a Fortune 500 company and often had grown men trembling in their boardroom chairs, was cooing and babbling like an idiot for his tiny baby girl. A complete and utter idiot.

Before Chad could even scan the rest of the group to see who was there, his eyes went to Jennie. She stuck her tongue out at him. He laughed and shook his head before grabbing a beer and joining her.

She stood talking to their friend Gabe Sawyer. Gabe owned a

string of hotels across the country and in several other countries as well, though Chad knew he'd started talking to Jack about possibly selling off some of his conglomerate.

Andrew and Jill walked up to join Jennie and Gabe at the same time Chad did.

He had no idea he could have so many warring emotions at once. He was relieved he and Jennie seemed to be back to being friends, even though he wanted a lot more than that. He was turned on beyond belief at the sight of her in the peach-colored sundress she wore, with her hair pulled up off her tanned shoulders.

Shoulders he wanted to touch and kiss and taste.

And he was fighting an internal rage at the fact that Gabe was standing there talking to his Jennie. No way in hell was he letting Gabe, a notorious womanizer, get anywhere near Jennie. The man traveled around the world, living in his hotels, entertaining a different woman every night.

Chad probably stood a little closer to Jennie than he should have, but he didn't want Gabe getting any ideas about chasing after her.

She cocked her head at him with that saucy little smile of hers as if to silently ask what he was doing. He let his eyes slide to Gabe for a split second but he saw Jennie pick up on his silent communication.

"Really, Big Man? Really?" she asked and laughed as she let incredulity seep into her voice.

"Wow. You two go away for two weeks and you're telepathic. You just had a whole conversation without us, didn't you?" Andrew asked

Chad and Jennie laughed. Andrew and Jack had cornered Chad after Florida, but he'd flat out lied to them. Told them nothing happened. The look on Andrew's face right now said he wasn't buying the lie. Time to redirect.

"Yeah. Jennie told me to do this," Chad said as he tossed Andrew into the pool with his clothes on.

Andrew managed to grab onto Chad's arm as he went into the water. Chad was struggling to right his balance on the edge of the pool when he felt two hands he recognized on his back.

The little vixen pushed him right in behind Andrew. Well, that took care of any unwanted attention on Jennie.

The whole group gathered around to laugh at Chad and Andrew as they wrestled in the pool. It had been too damn long since they'd done anything like this, Chad thought, as he shoved Andrew's head under the water again.

He was grinning like an idiot when Andrew grabbed his legs under the water, pulling him down and causing him to swallow a hell of a lot of pool water.

He didn't care. He was feeling better than he had since he and Jennie had returned from Florida. It felt good to be around his friends again, including Jennie. He would always want her. Always ache for her in a way that she clearly wouldn't ever ache for him. But, at least they could be around each other without being insanely uncomfortable.

If that was all he could have, he'd take it.

Jennie laughed as she watched Chad go under and come up with a mouthful of water. Of course her mind flashed to their time in Florida but she pushed those thoughts away.

Jennie knew she couldn't love Chad. Her heart belonged to Kyle. And, honestly, she really valued her friendship with Chad. She wanted to keep that.

If she gave in to what her body wanted again, she'd hurt him and lose him for good in the process. That wasn't something she was willing to do. From now on, she needed to stay in control of her body's response to him, no matter how strong the attraction was.

She turned away and took little Maddy in her arms when Kelly passed her over.

Losing herself in the baby's little coos and tiny smiles that were more likely caused by gas than genuine emotion, was just what Jennie needed.

She smiled down and made faces, watching in wonder as the baby's eyes went round in response.

She had heard somewhere that newborns were like little lumps, not really connecting with those around them until they were older.

Jennie thought that she'd either been completely misinformed, or Maddy must be a really special baby. She seemed to connect to everyone, always looking around with wide eyes as though taking in everything.

Jennie looked up and met Kelly's eyes. Her friend smiled back at her and Jennie felt nothing but contentment. She was happy for her friends. And happy she had so much love around her.

She might not be like the others. She wouldn't be finding her own happily ever after and starting a family like they were, but she had this. She had friendship and love and good people in her life. It would have to be enough.

CHAPTER 22

a month later, Jennie stared blankly at the screen on her computer. She wasn't actually seeing anything. She focused only on the mind-numbing reality of her situation as she blinked back tears. She was still in a state of shock. Still desperately trying to deny what she knew in her head was undeniable. Her heart, however, wasn't on board yet. Her heart had no interest in catching up to the facts.

Pregnant.

When she discovered last week that she had come home from Florida pregnant, she wanted to do nothing more than curl up in a ball and will it all away. Not the baby. But the last four years. And the way she felt about what she'd done.

She knew she had hurt Chad even though he tried to pretend she hadn't. She could see it in his eyes in quiet moments when he let his guard down. When he forgot to keep his walls up.

And, topping it all off, she'd betrayed Kyle in the worst way possible. Jennie had wanted to have Kyle's baby so desperately when he was alive. She had hoped for a baby with his sandy-blond hair and warm blue eyes.

She'd wanted a baby that had Kyle's smile and the dimple

that came out when he really grinned. When she knew he was smiling with all his heart.

She'd watched Kelly and Jack with Maddy. She'd held the baby often and saw how quickly she was growing and changing —all in such a short time. And seeing that was much harder than Jennie wanted to admit.

She needed to tell Chad about the baby, but how could she do that? Saying it out loud would make it real. If she said it out loud, she'd have to really face it. She didn't even have the guts to tell Kelly yet.

Right now, Zeke was the only one who knew her secret. He spent every moment shadowing her as if he knew something had changed and she'd spent several hours crying with her head buried in his soft fur. She'd told him everything, and he was the only one who she could trust to listen without judgment.

Add in the fact that she was so exhausted she could barely function and she'd begun to cry at the drop of a hat, and Jennie was officially an absolute basket case. A basket case with a baby she wanted, yet didn't want.

With a friend who would be a wonderful father to her baby. If only she wanted him to be. Which she didn't. It was horrible to think that, but the truth was, she didn't want Chad to be the baby's father.

Jennie lost the fight with the tears in that moment and had to make a dash for the bathroom. How could she hurt Chad this way? What would she tell her parents? Kyle's parents? How would she take care of a baby on her own when she was an emotional disaster?

This can't be happening.

But Jennie knew it was happening. She just didn't know what to do about it.

She splashed water on her face and took a few deep breaths. She should have called in today. Just like she should have called in sick yesterday and the day before. But, if she was home, she'd just cry again for hours on end. She needed to stop that.

She needed to find a way to just push through. To just keep going. She went back to her desk and tried to focus as if her world wasn't falling down around her. Again.

~

Chad sat at his desk and looked out the window but his eyes weren't seeing anything. As he had so many times in the past two months, he let his mind travel back to Florida, reliving every minute of his time with Jennie.

He tortured himself again and again, recalling the way she'd felt in his arms. How it felt to be able to reach over and hold her hand or pull her into his arms as they pretended to be newly-weds. How it felt to make her fall apart in his hands, with his mouth. And how it felt when he'd finally fulfilled a year of fantasies, sinking deep into Jennie's sweet depths and making love to her.

He even relived the moment on the plane ride home when she'd looked at him with those beautiful, guileless eyes and told him she was sorry she couldn't give him what he wanted.

He'd seen the regret in her eyes, had heard it in her voice. He knew she'd love him if she could. Or, at least, she'd try. She simply didn't have her heart to give. It still belonged to Kyle.

He'd told her it was okay. That he'd always be there for her and love her as a friend, no matter what. And, he'd meant it. He would always be there for Jennie. But, he knew the price he was going to pay for that.

It was tearing him to pieces, seeing her day in and day out at work. Seeing her on the weekends when they got together with friends. Watching her hold Jack and Kelly's baby girl. Fantasizing about a future they'd never have. About building a family with her. About things that would never come to be.

Chad spun in his chair and let his gaze fall on Jennie where she sat at her desk. She looked exhausted as he watched her in front of her computer and he wondered again if maybe she was sick. She hadn't looked good the last few days, but she showed up at work every day anyway.

Chad had the strongest urge to walk over and pull her into his arms. To carry her home and tuck her into bed. To care for her.

Those thoughts were interrupted by his phone.

"Yeah," Chad answered, pulling his eyes off Jennie.

"Chad, it's Jack."

He laughed. "You couldn't walk down the hall to talk to me? You had to call me?"

"Wise ass. I'm not in the building. I'm on my way to meet with the investors for the Paulsen project again. They need a little hand holding."

Chad grunted. He was glad Jack got to deal with the investors, not him. He didn't have it in him to handle people the way Jack did.

"I'm just calling to let you know I heard from Jonathan Masters. The FBI did exactly what you predicted. They sent the Masters brothers back in to gather info. They said they'd only cut them a deal if they collected enough information to indict the rest of the officials in the money laundering scheme," Jack said.

"Okay. Let's hope that means Jennie doesn't need to testify at all, or at least not for a long time," Chad said.

"I hope you're right about that, too. I'll see you this weekend at Jill and Andrew's, right?"

"Sure, I'll be there," Chad said, knowing it probably meant he'd see Jennie, too. He was beginning to dread seeing her at work and every weekend. Seeing her hurt like hell.

Chad crossed to his door and stuck his head out to the large area outside his office that held twenty desks spread through the room. He always thought of it as the bullpen.

"Jennie? Can I talk to you?" He called out across the room.

As he watched her approach, he couldn't help but notice how shaky she looked. Something wasn't right. He was positive. Only he didn't know what it was or why she wasn't telling him.

They'd been fine since they came home. Sure, the sexual tension that surrounded them was still there, but Chad knew it always would be. It wouldn't disappear simply because they'd decided not to act on it. If anything, it was worse after their one and only encounter.

But in the last week or two something had changed. Jennie wasn't herself.

"Shut the door," he said quietly when she walked in.

She shut the door and sat in one of the chairs in front of his desk crossing her legs and wrapping her arms around herself in an almost protective gesture. Instead of going around to the chair behind his desk, he sat beside her in the second guest chair. He studied her face but all he could see was exhaustion.

"You feel okay, Jennie? You look pretty pale."

"Mmm hmm." She nodded. "I think I've caught a little bug, but I'm okay. Just a little drained."

He didn't let up his stare as he assessed her. She was more than a little drained. She was pale and he could see dark circles under her eyes. She looked like she hadn't slept in days. Finally, he spoke.

"I wanted to fill you in on the investigation in Florida, but I want you to go home and rest after that. We don't need you for the rest of the day."

"I'm okay, Chad. I don't need to go home."

"Yeah, you do. You look like hell. I want you to go home."

She nodded. The fact that she didn't fight him too hard or have a wise-ass response told him how crappy she was feeling.

"It looks like you're off the hook for giving an official state-ment to the FBI for the moment, but I think they'll ask for one sooner or later. For now, they've sent the Masters brothers back in to gather evidence for them. Apparently, Rick Bandon has been on their radar for some time, but they've never been able to build a case. They had a guy come forward once after Bandon tried to extort money to make some problems on the guy's building site disappear, but the guy died in a suspicious accident a week later.

"I'm hoping you won't have to make a statement on the record yet, but I won't take any chances with you if it does come to that." Chad glanced to the door but then continued, leaning toward Jennie. "If it gets to that point, I want you to come stay at my place and let me protect you until you testify."

"Chad, no. I can't do that. You said yourself, it could take years for this to come to trial. I can't move in with you for years."

He almost had to laugh at the look of horror that crossed Jennie's face and stayed there at the idea of living with him. He probably would have laughed if it wasn't so damn sad. If his life hadn't become such a laughable joke.

He loved a woman who couldn't possibly love him back and he'd managed to put her in danger. She wanted so little to do with him that she wouldn't even let him protect her.

Before she could argue any further, she blanched and became even paler, if that were possible. Chad could swear she was about to pass out.

"Okay, I'm taking you home. Time for bed, Jen."

He was surprised when she didn't try her usual negotiation with him. She didn't put up a fight at all as he led her out of the office. He grabbed her purse and helped her out to his truck. She didn't even try to argue when he left her car at the office or during the car ride to her house—he could see how worn out she was.

He got her settled in bed with her Labrador, Zeke, babysitting her, and was walking down her front porch when it hit him. Something had been needling at Chad's brain for weeks. He froze as he realized what it was.

He knew Jennie's body like he knew his own. And her breasts were larger than they used to be. His mind flipped back to the

Sutton Capital softball team's game over the weekend. Jennie drank water instead of beer when they all went for pizza after the game. He remembered starting to pour her a beer, but she shook her head and pointed to her water. She'd shrugged it off when he raised an eyebrow.

Oh, Christ Jen.

Chad closed his eyes against the pain of knowing what Jennie was hiding from him. Such a small handful of details shouldn't be enough to tell him the truth, but he knew in his gut, he was right. Knew with certainty that Jennie was pregnant.

And, she hadn't come to him. Hadn't told him.

Oh, Jennie.

He sank down on the porch steps, head in his hands. Part of him wanted to storm back into the house and demand that she marry him.

But, he couldn't do that. Not to Jennie. Chad knew even the suggestion of marriage to someone other than Kyle would kill her.

Somehow, someway, Chad was going to have to come to grips with the fact that he wasn't going to be able to be with the woman who was having his baby. He wasn't going to be able to share a life with her the way he wanted to. Hell, he'd be lucky if she'd let him be a part of things at all.

CHAPTER 23

C had packed the last of the items in the extended cab of his truck. He was now ready to run with Jennie at a moment's notice with everything they'd need to stay off the grid for months.

He'd called some old friends and arranged for fake IDs for both of them. If anything came of this, and it looked like she was in danger, he'd keep her safe until she was ready to take the stand. If he had to, he'd relocate his whole life with her to keep her and the baby safe, both before and after the trial.

He hoped like hell he was overreacting. In fact, there was nothing more than his gut telling him he needed to be ready. As far as they knew, the Masters brothers were feeding the FBI evidence and would continue to do so until all of the people involved could be arrested. There was no reason to think Jennie would be in much danger from this.

But Chad trusted his gut. Listening to the creeping-finger feeling that walked up and down his spine had gotten him through a lot of tight scrapes in the military. He sure as hell wouldn't ignore that feeling when it involved Jennie.

At this point, his feelings for Jennie were a twisted mass of emotions he couldn't begin to unravel. He loved her more than he could have ever imagined loving someone other than his family. But he also hated her for keeping his child a secret from him. No, that wasn't true. It wasn't hate. It was an anger that coursed through his veins like poison.

When he was away from her, he seethed with anger. How could she be pregnant with his child and not tell him about it? He trusted that she would never do what Andrew's ex-girlfriend had done to him.

She would never abort the baby without telling him. He knew Jennie and knew she didn't have that in her to do. But as the week dragged on, and Jennie didn't come to him, his fury built.

Until he saw her. Whenever he saw Jennie, the anger drained away and hopelessness took over. He didn't know how to help her. She looked so lost. She was hurting more than he could imagine.

Whenever he saw her, he realized that it must be killing her to be having a child with a man who wasn't her husband. The husband he knew in his heart she still loved.

And, so he waited. She would come to him eventually. He knew that. She just needed time.

In the meantime, he planned. He had cash ready to go. Burner phones. Clothes for both of them. Dog food and a crate for Zeke. And a remote cabin. If the time came, Chad wouldn't trust Jennie's safety to anyone other than himself.

"M-m-matt, w-w-w-we can't keep doing this. Bandon knows something. I can f-f-f-feel it." Alan looked down right miserable and his stutter became more pronounced each day.

Matt knew his brother was right. Bandon hadn't sent them any more money recently and he was avoiding all talk of business other than boat trips and dock rental on the phone.

The FBI was pressuring them for more information, for

evidence they could use to track the other people involved in the money laundering, but Bandon wasn't falling for anything.

"Don't worry little brother," Matt said, trying to calm Alan down. If Alan panicked, things would only get worse. Matt was always the one to take care of things. To fix things. He would do it now. He'd hold things together long enough for them to get the evidence they needed to get the FBI off their backs and then they'd move on.

He had been stashing money here and there for years. He had enough money for him and Alan to start over someplace. They wouldn't live the way they had been, living it up in the sun, but they'd be alive. And, not in prison.

"I'll figure out a way to get the agents what they need."

"H-h-h—" His brother stopped, his frustration palpable as he struggled to ask the question.

Matt didn't need to hear the question. Alan was going to ask him how they'd do that. Alan hated it when Matt finished sentences for him instead of giving him time to get the words out himself, but he couldn't help himself right now.

Alan wanted to know how. And, he had no idea how he would take care of things. How he would get the evidence they needed.

He had already given the FBI the records they had, but they weren't satisfied with that. They'd noticed the bigger numbers coming in lately, just as the brothers had. They wanted to know the same thing Matt had wondered himself.

Who was the other money being laundered for? Mafia? Other government officials? Maybe other housing inspectors. Who knew? The possibilities were endless, really.

"I don't know, brother," he said now to Alan, ignoring the unspoken rule not to answer questions his brother hadn't managed to spit out. "I'll think of something, though."

He'd tried telling Bandon he knew there was more money coming than Bandon himself could need laundered. He had demanded to know where the money was coming from.

Bandon had acted like he hadn't even asked the questions. He'd just kept right on talking about the boat business and refused to answer a thing. But, Matt would come up with something. He had to. He and Alan couldn't go to prison over this. They just couldn't.

CHAPTER 24

C had got the call three days later. The FBI had lost track of the Masters brothers. They missed their last two check-ins with their handler and hadn't been spotted since then. They were missing in the wind and no one had any idea where Rick Bandon had gone either.

Something felt very wrong to Chad. And, he wasn't going to wait around to see what happened. He made calls to Jack and Andrew as he headed over to Jennie's. It was time to get her out of town. Time to be sure she was safe.

Jennie opened the door to a very intense-looking Chad. He didn't wait for an invitation or even for her to step out of his way. He pushed his way into her house and dropped his duffle bag on the floor.

Zeke didn't bat an eye at Chad's pushy entrance. He knew Chad and apparently didn't consider him an intruder.

Jennie eyed her 'faithful' dog with a raised brow.

Traitor.

"Gee, Chad. Please, come in. Mi casa is apparently su casa," she said with her typical bite of sarcasm.

All she wanted to do was crawl into bed. It might only be nine o'clock at night but her body was done. She needed sleep. Jennie couldn't get over how tired this pregnancy was making her.

Kelly had told her how tired she was when she was pregnant with Maddy, but Jennie had no idea it would be this bad. She walked around in a constant fog as though her head were a block of mush not a brain.

"The Masters brothers are missing. I'm your new protection detail." In a move completely uncharacteristic of him, he kicked off his shoes, dropped his large body onto Jennie's small couch, and put his feet up on the coffee table.

She didn't know why he was acting so out of character, but she just wanted him to leave so she could go to bed.

"Chad, I don't need protection. My name isn't even on the record with the FBI yet. They have a whole investigation to do before my testimony even becomes a possibility."

She crossed to the door and opened it, waiting for him to leave.

Naturally, he didn't budge.

"Listen, Hulk, I'd love to have a slumber party and wax our legs, braid each other's hair and all that, but that's not happening tonight. I'm too tired. You need to go."

"The hell I do. You'll have to get over this, Jennie. The Masters brothers know you heard something and when their uncle showed up with a lawyer a few days later I'm sure they put two and two together. I'm not taking a chance that they know about you or that they might have told Rick Bandon about you. Until we know where they are, I'm not going anywhere. You're going to have protection whether you like it or not. Whether it's me or someone else."

Oh, enough is enough. What the hell?

Jennie was more than a little annoyed at this point. She sure as hell couldn't share a house with Chad. Not now. Not until she figured out what to do about the baby. Not until she was ready to tell him what was going on.

Never?

"Chad, I told you—"

In the split second before he rose from the couch, Jennie saw something she had never seen in his face before.

Unbridled anger. Anger he wasn't trying to cover or calm or neutralize the way he usually did. The man who was always in control was suddenly, very much out of control and coming at her full force and there wasn't anything funny about it.

She swallowed her words and stepped back as Chad filled the space in front of her.

"You're having my fucking baby, Jennie!" Chad bellowed. "I'll protect you for as long as I damn well please in whatever way I damn well please."

Her heart stopped in her chest, frozen. She stood, eyes wide, speechless for several minutes as she watched him regain control.

She could feel the tears coming and she clenched her jaw to try to stop them as she watched Chad coil back all of the rage he had let loose moments before, until his mask was back in place.

A lump formed in her throat at the effort of holding back the tears and she knew she was seconds away from losing the battle. Regret was a tight ball in her stomach, making her sick with the what ifs and if onlies of the entire situation.

When he spoke again he was quiet. Controlled. But the anger was there. She could feel it pouring off him in waves just under the surface.

"Did you think I wouldn't figure it out? Did you think I wouldn't notice? That I don't know you better than you know yourself, Jennie?" Chad's words spat from his mouth and Jennie recoiled.

There was nothing she could say, she realized. Nothing to make him forgive her for this. He would hate her, and she honestly couldn't blame him one bit. She hated herself right then.

"How did you know?" Her voice sounded quiet, almost foreign to her own ears.

His smirk was bitter. "I observe, Jennie. It's what I do. You should know that better than anyone. I saw how tired you were. You're run down all the time. Just like Kelly was."

His gaze fell to her breasts, and Jennie had to purposefully resist the urge to cross her arms over them. She knew they were slightly bigger than they used to be. But, how the hell could he know that?

"At first, I thought you must be sick but then I noticed the difference in your body. I know every inch of you, remember, Jen?"

He always said 'Jen' so playfully, almost intimately. This time, it shot out of his mouth like the taste of it was bitter on his tongue and she winced.

"You're not gaining weight yet, but your body has changed."

She shook her head, trying to clear the fogginess she felt all the time now. Trying to make this all go away.

She raised her chin a notch. "What makes you think the baby is yours?" It was probably the wrong tactic to try to deny what they both knew was true, but she wasn't ready to share her secret yet. She wasn't ready for anyone to know, even him. She hadn't even told Kelly yet.

His face fell. With a sad defeated voice, he spoke what they both knew couldn't be denied. "Because you haven't been with anyone but me, Jennie."

She shook her head, hanging on to the denial as long as she could. "You don't know that. You don't—"

"I do, Jen." He reached out, brushing his fingertips down her cheek, causing a shiver of longing for what she couldn't have. "I do know, Jen, because it damn near killed you just to be with me."

Chad let his hand drop to his side and stepped back from her.

He crossed to the couch and lay on it, arms behind his head, feet propped on the arm because they wouldn't fit on the couch itself.

He didn't look at her. Only closed his eyes. She knew he was done talking.

"Go to sleep, Jennie. Just go to sleep."

CHAPTER 25

*S*pecial Agent Burke of the FBI, the agent in charge of the Bandon investigation in Florida, called Chad at seven the next morning to let him know the Masters brothers had been found. They were both dead and neither death had been easy.

Rick Bandon was spotted on video at the airport in Hartford, Connecticut. They didn't have a clue where the man had gone after that.

Chad threw off the aches and pains from his night on the couch and sat up. Hartford was much too close to Jennie for his comfort.

There was no way in hell it was a coincidence the guy was here. As he called quietly to Zeke, luring the dog out of Jennie's bed with sausage treats, he dialed Jack's number.

When Jack answered, Chad could hear the sound of a crying baby in the background. He felt a sharp pain as the thought crossed his mind that Jennie might not let him raise his baby with her. She might not want him to be a part of their lives.

Screw that. I'll raise my child with her no matter what.

Chad shoved aside those thoughts. He needed to get Jennie

out of there. He snapped a leash on Zeke and took the dog outside as he talked to his cousin.

"Jack, I'm taking Jennie away for a while. The Masters brothers are dead. Tortured and shot. Rick Bandon is missing but he was last seen in Connecticut."

"I don't like the sound of that. Could he have found out about Jennie?"

"I don't know, but I'm not taking any chances. The Masters brothers knew someone had found evidence that forced their uncle to come to them and get them to turn themselves in. It would be easy for them to narrow it down to Jennie and me after they ran into her outside their office.

"When their uncle showed up two days later with a lawyer, they had to suspect it was us. We used our real names for that trip. I'm not taking any chances. I've got everything set in place. I'll call you from a burner phone when we get where we're going. But, listen, Jack, I don't know how long we'll be gone."

Chad and Jennie worked with three others in the small investigations department at Sutton. If they were both out for months, that could really screw things up.

"Don't even think about that. Keeping Jennie safe is your only job right now. And, make sure she knows her job is secure no matter how long she's gone. We'll manage until you get back."

"Can you send Andrew out to Jennie's parents' place to let them know what's going on? I don't want her to tell them by phone but they need to know she's safe." As he spoke, Chad opened his truck to let Zeke, who had now had a potty break, jump into the cab. He took off the leash, shut the door and walked back into the house.

"Yeah. I'll send him out there this morning. Kelly knows where they live."

"Go in the bottom drawer of my desk at the office. There are two bags of burner phones. The top bag is for you and Kelly and the bottom bag is for Jennie's parents. I've got the numbers for all of them so we can reach you when we need to. Make sure Jennie's parents know they need to throw the phone away in a dumpster or public trash can after they use it. We'll only use each phone for a week or two at a time and then get rid of it," Chad instructed.

"Got it. Be careful, Chad," Jack said.

"Always," Chad said with a grin he didn't feel and then he ended the call.

He tossed his phone on the kitchen counter and grabbed Jennie's purse. He dug for her phone and pulled it out. She had several missed calls from a number Chad recognized immediately. Agent Burke.

Shit.

He was willing to bet Burke would be pushing for Jennie to make a statement now and Chad didn't want her talking to anyone about what she saw until Rick Bandon was in custody. He tossed her phone on the counter with his. He had five burner phones waiting for them in the car.

They were taking his truck but he had an extra set of plates that couldn't be traced back to him. They'd get out of town and then stop and put the new plates on. He had everything in place.

Now to deal with the little hellcat in the bedroom who probably wouldn't go with him willingly.

Chad stood at the foot of the bed and watched Jennie sleep. He hated to wake her, but they needed to get on the road. He pondered how to get a pregnant woman to the car.

He'd normally toss her over his shoulder but that was out since he didn't want to put any pressure on her stomach. She wasn't showing yet, but he had no clue what could or couldn't hurt the baby at this stage, and he wasn't taking chances.

He finally slipped his arms under her shoulders and legs, lifting her in a cradle hold. If he held her tightly, she shouldn't be able to slip away.

She came awake groggily and looked up at him. "Chad?" Her brow furrowed with confusion but he could also see the exhaustion evident in her face. When they got to the cabin, he needed to find out if this level of fatigue was normal for someone at her stage of pregnancy. She seemed too tired, too sick. And, that scared the hell out of him.

"Time to hit the road, Jen. Rick Bandon may be headed this way and I'm pretty sure he has your name. You and I are going away for a bit until the feds can pick him up," Chad said as they moved quickly through her small house and out the front door.

"What? No! Put me down, Chad. You can't do this!" She kicked and squirmed in his arms but he held tight.

Oh, shit.

Old Mrs. Stempski was out on her porch in her bathrobe, newspaper in hand, watching as Chad forcibly removed Jennie from her house.

Not good.

"Hi, Mrs. Stempski! How are you this morning?" Chad called out cheerfully as he pinned Jennie's arms with a tighter grip.

"Is everything all right, Jennie?" the nosy busybody asked.

"Oh sure. Dentist appointment," he said. "She does this every time."

"I do not! Call the police, Mrs. Stempski! He's kidnapping me!"

Chad put Jennie down in front of the passenger side door, holding her tightly with one arm as he swatted her ass with the other. "Knock it off. You're going whether you like it or not."

He smiled again at Mrs. Stempski. "She's terrified of drills and shots."

Zeke barked excitedly from the back seat as if he were going on a fun trip, apparently unconcerned that his mistress was being carted off against her wishes.

"Some watchdog," Jennie mumbled.

"You listen to that boy, Jennie, and let him take you to the dentist. You have to take care of your teeth, dear!"

Chad barely suppressed a laugh at the look of shock on

page 130, LORI RYAN

Jennie's face when Mrs. Stempski not only bought his story, but began to lecture Jennie about proper oral hygiene. It was pretty comical.

He put Jennie in the truck and buckled her in, ignoring the rush his already ridiculously turned-on body felt when his arm grazed her chest.

As Chad rounded the front of his truck, he kept the key chain pointed at the truck. Jennie unlocked the electronic locks; he locked them. She unlocked them again; he locked them.

Now how to unlock them fast enough to get in and then lock them again without her getting out? *Shit.* He'd have to get her to go along with his plan somehow. He crossed back over to her side and opened her door, blocking her escape with his body.

Speaking quietly so Mrs. Stempski couldn't hear, he did the only thing he could think to do to get her to come along. He scared the hell out of her. It fucking gutted him to do it, but it was better than getting a call that she'd been killed.

"Jen, the Masters brothers were found dead. They were tortured and then shot in the head. This Bandon guy isn't screwing around. I know you'll never love me the way I love you, Jennie. And I'll find a way to live with that. But, I won't lose you, and I won't lose our baby. You are leaving with me now, whether you like it or not."

Jennie stilled and watched him wide eyed. He hated to scare her like that, but she needed to understand what they were up against. She needed to know the truth so he could protect her.

She nodded her head, saying nothing, but he knew she'd acquiesced. She would let him protect her, at least for the time being. He let out the breath he'd been holding and shut the door, then raised a hand to wave at Mrs. Stempski.

He pulled away from Jennie's home, not at all sure when or if he'd ever be able to bring her back to it.

CHAPTER 26

*J*ennie stared out at the yellow lines of the road. It seemed they'd passed miles and miles of them. She finally cleared her throat to break the uneasy silence that filled the cab of Chad's truck.

"Where are we going?" she asked. She kept her head against the window, facing away from the man who was her friend, a lover of sorts, the father of her baby—and now, quite possibly, her savior.

"A cabin in New Hampshire. I rented it a couple of weeks ago under a fake name and paid cash. It's near a small town so we'll have access to anything we need, but secluded enough that we won't run into people much. When that lease is up, we'll move to another secluded spot."

"No room service?" Jennie let a teasing tone enter her voice but the sadness, the shock over what was happening was still there. She could hear it, and she knew he would, too.

She got a laugh out of Chad though. "Sorry. Not this time. I have a few dry things packed in the back. Cereal bars, juice boxes, dog food for Zeke. We'll stock up on more when we get there."

"I don't have any clothes," Jennie said almost to herself as she realized she was in the shorts and T-shirt she'd slept in.

"I packed you some last week. I came in while you were at work and packed a bag full of stuff from the back of your closet that you wouldn't notice was missing. Mostly dresses so you can wear them later in the pregnancy," Chad said.

She turned to her traitorous dog that lay sleeping in the backseat. "Do you let everyone walk in when I'm not home?"

Chad laughed. "Only people with sausage treats. We'll get you some new clothes eventually. I brought enough cash for us to manage for a while. Jack plans to use my credit card around town and I'll call Kelly and have her get one of your cards from your house and use it. If Burke runs our cards it will look like we're still in town."

Jennie looked down at her purse on the floor. "You left my credit cards at my house?"

"Yes. And your phone. I have disposable phones for us. Andrew's driving over to see your parents today. He'll fill them in. Make sure they know you're safe. He'll bring them disposable phones so we can call them later to let them know we got to the cabin safely."

"How do you know how to do all this, Chad? Why do I get the feeling you could make us disappear forever if you needed to?"

Chad didn't answer her. He kept his eyes locked on the road.

"I think you owe me at least that much, Chad. Tell me what's going on."

He rolled his eyes. "You know how I served three tours as an Army Ranger?"

"Uh huh," Jennie said, watching him. They all knew about his time in the military.

"I didn't."

"Excuse me? What? You...what?" She sputtered.

"I did eight years in the military as a Ranger. The rest of the time my family thought I was serving overseas, I was working for a private company. I hooked up with three of the men I served with after I was honorably discharged. We did freelance work around the world."

"A mercenary! You were a mercenary!" Her eyes practically bugged out of her head.

He laughed. "No. I mean, technically, I guess you could call it that, but we did a lot of work extracting people from dangerous places. We were occasionally hired to rescue people who'd been kidnapped, and other times we helped people disappear when they needed to. We could do things the U.S. military couldn't do. But, I swear, we got paid enough that we were able to be selective. We could pick and choose who we wanted to work for and we always made sure we were on the right side."

Jennie shook her head, unable to process what he'd told her. He really could make her disappear as long as she needed to. She could hide forever if these people came after her.

The enormity of the situation was hitting home a little at a time, but things still felt a bit insane to Jennie. Okay, a lot insane.

How could this be happening? It wasn't enough that she was pregnant. That the baby inside her wasn't her husband's. Now she might have a crooked building inspector after her? On what planet does this happen? Because it wasn't supposed to be happening on hers.

"How long will we stay at the cabin?" Jennie asked.

"We have it the rest of the summer. If this isn't resolved by then, we'll switch locations."

She looked at him for a long time. "Fine. But, if we change locations, I get a say in the next place. You can't take over my life. If we do this, we're doing it together from now on." She tried to sound firm, even though she guessed he could see right through her to the shaky uncertainty she was swimming in.

Chad nodded and she wondered if he'd really let her have any say in where they went or how they hid or how long they stayed in hiding.

She watched him from the corner of her eye and could see the tension in his body. The pain in his eyes. God, how she hated what she was doing to him. How she was hurting him. And would continue to hurt him.

He was giving up his life, his job, his friends and family for her. And she hadn't even told him about his baby.

She couldn't stop the tears that came as everything she was feeling began to hit at once. They streamed down her face full force and much faster than she could get control over things.

She owed this man so much "I'm sorry, Chad. I'm so sorry I didn't tell you about the baby. I only needed to be alone with it for a while longer. I just needed to think, without anyone knowing. It's confusing, you know? And if I told anyone, it made it real. I just wasn't ready for it to be real."

Chad glanced at her. "Aw, Jen. Don't cry, honey." He reached over and threaded his fingers through her hair, brushing the tears from her face with his thumb.

Jennie waved off his concern and brushed away the tears with the backs of her hands. "Ignore this. I cry at the drop of a hat now. It's the hormones. I cry over the printer being out of paper at work, and the birds chirping outside my window and waking me up too early, and the fact that I can't drink coffee anymore."

And how much I miss Kyle and want him here with me. How much I wish you could hold me but I can't ask you to do that because it's not fair to you. I cry over how much I'm hurting you.

She couldn't say any of that to him. There was so much that couldn't be said between them.

He was quiet for a while as the truck ate up the road and Jennie reigned in her tears. When he spoke, there was a steely resolve to his tone.

"I will be a part of the baby's life, Jen. I know you wish it wasn't mine, but I won't walk away from my baby."

Jennie closed her eyes and nodded. "I know." She wouldn't expect any less of him.

She didn't know how they'd negotiate this one and what they'd work out, but she knew regardless of what they agreed on, there would be a lot of pain for both of them in the months to come.

CHAPTER 27

*B*eing together at the cabin was much harder than sharing the villa at the resort. In the cabin, they were isolated with no one around to buffer their interactions. Jennie and Zeke slept in the only bedroom while Chad slept in the living area on a cot outside her door. The cramped kitchen and small bathroom made up the rest of the space.

They cooked meals together instead of going to restaurants. They washed and dried the dishes together and went to the grocery store. They did laundry and all of the other mundane domestic things that couples did.

When they first arrived, Chad saw that the light that usually surrounded Jennie had gone out. She wasn't happy and laughing like she used to.

Oh, he had always known that there was some sadness in Jennie. But, despite the scars she carried, Jennie had been happy before all this. She'd been the one to joke around. She was a smart ass. She was bold and edgy and impertinent. She never showed him an ounce of respect on the outside as her boss, but he knew she respected him just the same.

It was hard to explain, but it was the way she was. The way they had been, until the Florida job.

Now, there was no lightheartedness in her. By giving in to his enormous need to be close to Jennie, he'd been the one to take all that from her. He should have talked to Jack as soon as he suspected the reason behind the Florida trip. He shouldn't have let Jennie get on that plane with him.

He should have considered the consequences and said no when she asked him for one night. And, when he didn't have the strength to say no, he should have made damn sure he had a condom on before he went anywhere near her.

Those few minutes in the shower when he'd slipped up and taken her without protection had cost Jennie so much. His lapse was costing her whatever bit of happiness she'd managed to find after Kyle's death.

He was also concerned about her pregnancy.

On their first trip to the store, Chad bought a copy of that *What to Expect* pregnancy book. He read to Jennie from it sometimes when they were sitting and watching television or rocking in the side-by-side rockers on the front porch.

He had to admit, that book turned him into the pregnancy police. He monitored Jennie's intake of fruits and veggies, even though many days, it was all she could do to keep toast down. Jennie craved pastries so he bought her oranges.

"Where is the logic in that? What do oranges have to do with pastries?" she would ask him.

"Eat an orange and I'll go get you pastries," Chad would say to her some days.

Instead of negotiating and saying, "I'll eat half an orange," like he expected her to, Jennie had given him the hell-hath-no-fury-like-a-pregnant-woman-without-her-pastry look and countered, "I'll eat an orange if you carry the baby for the rest of the pregnancy. How about that? Now get me my damned pastries."

Yeah. Their negotiation tactics had changed somewhat lately.

Slowly, she began to build up that outer façade of happiness with him again. She joked more, even when her head was in the toilet bowl puking up whatever he got her to eat.

She yelled at him for feeding Zeke table scraps but would laugh when he said he wanted to stay in Zeke's good graces so the dog would take his side in any arguments with Jennie.

In the afternoons, when her morning sickness had subsided, they went for walks together in the woods. Zeke would run around them off leash and Jennie would laugh and chitchat with Chad, acting much more like the Jennie he had fallen for.

Chad could almost pretend everything was normal and she wasn't gutted inside.

~

They were in a holding pattern, waiting for Jack to call with news from Agent Burke. They'd only been able to talk to Jack and Kelly and to Jennie's parents once when they first arrived.

Jack reported that Jennie's house had been broken into and trashed. Someone had been there looking for her or for signs of her whereabouts.

Jennie knew the danger she was facing but she still wished she could talk to Kelly and Jill. She hadn't told any of them about the baby and neither had Chad. It had been a week since they arrived at the cabin and Jennie was getting tired of watching TV, playing card games, and taking walks with Zeke in the woods.

The hardest part, and the thing that Jennie couldn't understand, was that after all that had happened—including being ten weeks pregnant and having a money-laundering building inspector after her—Jennie was still so turned on by Chad she could barely breathe. Shouldn't the pregnancy slow down her libido? She'd never been so freaking aroused in her life.

And seeing Chad every day after his morning run with Zeke didn't help. He came back sweating, with his T-shirt clinging to that godlike chest of his. He'd strip the shirt off and jump into the lake to cool off.

He probably had no idea she watched him through the kitchen window—actually stood there timing herself to his routines every day to be sure she didn't miss it. Then he'd walk out of the lake dripping wet, with beads of water running over his shoulders and his wet hair looking even darker than it was.

Oh, God.

Jennie curled her feet up under her on the couch as she tried to banish the slide show playing in her mind's eye. She needed to learn to ignore the way her body reacted to Chad. She needed to get her body in line with what her head and her heart wanted.

As if he could read her mind, Chad chose that very moment to look up from his *What to Expect* book.

"Says here some women get really horny when they're pregnant," he said, waggling his eyebrows with a shit-eating grin.

"It does not!" Jennie said, feeling two hot spots form on her cheeks.

How does he know?

"Does too. They don't phrase it that way, but that's essentially it. Anything you need help with, Jennie? Any *cravings* I can take care of for you?" He laughed as he leaned in suggestively.

"Gah!" She stood and stormed off to the shower, not looking back at him as she went into the bathroom.

She gave in to the urge to rearrange his neatly laid out toiletries on the counter by the sink, though. It was an activity she allowed herself to indulge in at least once a week to keep her sanity. Mussing up his ordered tidiness helped her feel a little better about his teasing.

It didn't do anything to diffuse the insane arousal she was fighting at the moment, though. Chad had her so wound up, she felt like she would burst soon. Her heart raced and she had the sweet achiness of need between her legs almost twenty-four hours a day.

And, no amount of self-indulgence seemed to quell her hunger for Chad. If anything, it seemed to make it worse.

Jennie sighed as she turned Chad's razor perpendicular to his toothpaste and moved his toothbrush over to the other side of the sink, then stepped into the shower. She knew better than to hope a cold shower would help, and truth be told, she didn't have it in her to take one.

She needed the comfort of the warm water beating down on her nowadays. Her life had become one long twisted joke lately and she didn't have any idea when it was going to change.

She put her hand to her belly and tried to imagine the tiny life that was growing there. This poor child was going to come into a mixed-up mess of a situation and Jennie didn't know how to change that.

She closed her eyes and stepped beneath the spray remembering a shower in Florida that started all of this. She rubbed her hand over her belly again. She couldn't regret the baby, but she did worry that she wasn't going to be able to give the little one anything resembling the kind of life she should.

She squeezed her eyes shut. *What have I done?*

CHAPTER 28

C had waited for Jennie to turn off the water in the shower before knocking on the door.

"Jennie," he said through the door. "Dinner—chicken or beef?"

"Cheese danish," came her reply.

"Uh, no. Chicken, then. Stir-fry chicken with veggies or grilled chicken and salad?"

She opened the door, letting out a cloud of steam with her. Chad looked down at her, hair wet, bathrobe around her tiny frame, and her hands fisted on her hips as if she were ready to take him on.

She smelled of that light flowery scent he was pretty sure was lilacs, but also seemed innately Jennie. Her body still glistened with beads of water and he had to fight the urge to lean down and lick at the droplets.

His body's response to her was involuntary and unwelcome, but it was there just the same. There was no stopping it.

He only hoped he could ignore it and that she didn't notice. He knew, if she asked, he would probably give her anything she wanted.

Except cheese danish for dinner.

"Pudding, then. I'll have pudding," Jennie said.

She brushed past him and either didn't see his eye roll or chose to ignore it.

"Jennie, you can't just eat shit like that. You need more nutrients in you."

Chad could tell she wasn't eating nearly enough to feed both herself and the baby. As much as he didn't want to be angry with her, his frustration was wearing on him. He wanted to strap her to a chair and force-feed her something more than pudding, but he forced his expression into a neutral mask.

"I puke up more nutrients. I can keep pudding and pastries down. If I eat anything else I throw it up. My doctor said not to worry about it for now. The nausea should stop in a couple of weeks. Then I can eat all the fruits and veggies and lean protein you want to shove in me. But for right now, she said to eat whatever I can keep down. I can keep down pudding and pastries. So, you choose. Either one is fine with me."

Her grin was cheeky, but Chad didn't want to give in, no matter how cute she looked when she argued with him. He hated that she was so sick at times and he was beginning to wonder if this was normal.

There were times when she was retching on what he knew had to be an empty stomach and he wondered if the baby could be harmed from that. It couldn't be good for the baby. He read his way through most of the book on pregnancy and realized nausea was pretty standard but he'd feel even better if she saw a doctor.

"Hey, Jen. We could be here awhile. Maybe we need to find a doctor in this area to see you. Aren't you supposed to go in for regular visits now?" he asked.

She stopped pulling clothes out of her dresser and looked at him.

"My next visit isn't for a couple more weeks. I don't have to go in very often right now, but as things progress, I'll have to go more regularly." She stopped and furrowed her brow. "Wouldn't we need to give them my real name and show ID if we go to someone here, though?"

Chad shook his head. "No. A walk-in clinic would only check ID if we were using insurance. We'll pay cash."

Jennie nodded. "Okay. We'll go soon," she said and went back into the bathroom to get dressed.

"I'll go start the pudding," he said wryly as he left the room.

He was sure she was losing weight instead of gaining. Chad shoved down the irritation, knowing it wasn't her fault she couldn't keep healthy food down. His urge to fix things, to make everything all better for her, was overwhelming. Because, it seemed, as hard as he tried, he couldn't fix this for Jennie. He couldn't take care of her and the baby if he couldn't even figure out how to get her to keep food down. And that knowledge ate at him.

The sharp metallic smell of blood and the cruel odor of twisted, burned flesh invaded Chad's nose, bringing him back to consciousness with a start. Chopper blades sounded overhead, letting him know his men would get to safety. An extraction team would get them out.

The pressure and pain in Chad's chest penetrated the cloud in his head. He struggled for a full breath of air, but none came. He couldn't fill his lungs.

Chad turned his head to a medic crouched by his side—the man's shirt was covered in blood. The medic spoke to Chad, but the noise of the helicopter drowned out the sound. His lips moved, but nothing came out. The needle he was pushing into Chad's chest drew all of his attention as the pain came alive.

He turned his head away from the pain, but immediately wished he hadn't. Jennie lay beside him, her body limp and life-less, her eyes open but no longer seeing. Chad struggled to get up, but his body was frozen. He couldn't move to help her. He cried out to her, but she didn't move.

He was panicked and weak with fear as he realized Jennie's body was covered in blood, a gaping hole in her stomach where his baby, their baby should be.

"Jennie!"

He struggled to move, then turned to yell at the medic to help her, but the man just kept talking calmly to Chad as if nothing was wrong. As though he couldn't see that Jennie needed him. That she needed to be saved.

"Jennie!" He called to her again and again, but she didn't open her eyes. She didn't turn to him. She didn't move at all.

"Chad! Chad!" Jennie's voice sounded miles away and it wasn't coming from her body beside him. Something was wrong. Her voice came at him through a thick fog, as if she were trying to draw him back to her from somewhere far away.

He opened his eyes with a start, heart pounding against his ribs. Jennie stood at the foot of his cot, as though she knew better than to get too close while he was having a nightmare, but wanting to be near.

He was drenched in sweat, his thin T-shirt stuck to his chest as his pulse raced. He wiped a hand down his face, trying to erase his mind's image of Jennie covered in blood, their baby gone.

He focused on the willowy cotton gown she wore and the way tendrils of her hair fell over her breasts.

He reached out his hand, wanting to feel her, to know she was real and alive and whole, that she was still with him. She crawled onto the cot and wrapped her arms around him, holding him close.

He held tightly to her, knowing he shouldn't but not willing to let her go. He breathed in her scent and listened to the murmured words of comfort she whispered in his ear for what seemed like hours.

When he woke later, his arms were empty. Chad sat up and

looked at the light pouring in the windows of the cabin, falling on the floor of the living room.

Morning.

He sat on the edge of the cot and wondered how much he had dreamt and how much was real. He wasn't sure if Jennie had come to him after his nightmare or if he'd just wanted her to be there so much, he'd conjured her up.

He held a hand out in front of him, not surprised to see that it shook. Seeing Jennie in his dream, her body so still and lifeless, had shaken him more than any of the horrors he'd seen in war.

He rose and went to the door of Jennie's room to make sure she was okay. She lay sleeping, more beautiful than he remembered. Her hair fanned out on the pillow and her arms wrapped around Zeke. She looked so small and frail. Not like the Jennie he was used to seeing.

He began to wonder how her tiny body was going to manage to carry a baby that could someday be his size, but he turned away and forced the worry from his mind. He needed to get a handle on his paranoia. He wouldn't make it through the pregnancy if he kept this up.

Chad walked to the kitchen and began searching through drawers and cupboards. He would bet they'd have a good old-fashioned phone book around the cabin somewhere. He needed to find a walk-in clinic to get Jennie checked out. He had to know she and the baby were okay.

Three hours later, they walked into the small medical clinic two towns over from where the cabin was located. If they were holed up there much longer, Chad would find a doctor he was sure they could trust with Jennie's real name and medical history. For right now, he wanted someone who wouldn't check the fake IDs he carried in his pocket, or at least wouldn't push too hard if they thought they were fake. He wanted to be sure Jennie and the baby were okay.

He would pay cash, giving them no reason to even ask for ID, much less question it. The clinic probably often saw people who lied about their names for one reason or another. He didn't much care if they did pick up on their fake names.

In fact, he didn't care if they thought he was her drug dealer or her pimp, as long as they made sure Jennie was okay. He'd been watching her lose weight. The few times he'd gotten her to eat anything other than pudding or pastries, he ended up holding her hair for her while she threw it up. Then he'd watch her try to smile and joke about how she felt, faking her good spirits when he could tell she was getting more and more drained.

He didn't understand how her body could handle a croissant but not chicken or pasta. And, he hated that he couldn't fix it for her. He should be taking better care of them, he told himself.

After filling out forms and answering a few questions, they sat side by side in ragged chairs in the clinic's waiting room. Chad reached over and laced his fingers through hers. She stared straight ahead but she did squeeze his hand back. He knew this had to suck for her.

Going to some walk-in clinic instead of to the doctor she knew and trusted. And being in a strange cabin out in the woods when she felt so sick and tired all the time, instead of being in her own bed. Being pregnant with his baby when she probably wished with all her heart it was Kyle's baby.

A door opened on the far side of the room and a woman in scrubs held the door open.

"Nancy?"

Chad had to squeeze Jennie's hand to get her to respond to the fake name. She stood and crossed to the door, but paused when she got there, turning back to him.

"Come with me?"

He felt his heart kick into high gear and he wondered for a second if he'd heard her right. Maybe he'd imagined it? He couldn't believe she asked him to be with her for the exam. Chad had planned to ask if he could be there for one of her ultrasounds down the road, but he never thought she'd want him to come in with her this time.

He rose and went through the door with Jennie, taking her hand in his again. The nurse stopped off at a bathroom and asked Jennie to leave a urine sample. He saw the flush in her cheeks and wondered if she was sorry she had brought him back there.

When she emerged from the bathroom, they were shown to a small room. They didn't ask Jennie to undress so he wasn't sure whether she would be given a full exam or not.

An older woman walked in the room and introduced herself as Dr. Breckman. She listened as Jennie filled her in on how far along she was, her exhaustion and nausea and inability to eat anything other than pudding and pastries.

"Well, let's take a listen to the baby and make sure things sound good, then we can talk about getting more food in you," Dr. Breckman said with a kind smile.

The woman didn't seem overly concerned, which made Chad alternate between feeling relieved and wondering if he should shake the woman and yell until her level of concern matched his.

The doctor pulled out a small handheld machine and helped Jennie lay back on the exam table. She lifted Jennie's shirt and tucked the top of Jennie's jeans under a bit to get to her lower abdomen. She squirted clear gel on her stomach. This is when it dawned on Chad that the doctor had said they'd be listening to the baby's heartbeat.

He was going to hear his baby's heartbeat for the first time. He felt his own heartbeat kick into high gear with anticipation. Somehow, the baby had seemed almost theoretical before. Now, it was about to be very real.

"Have you lost weight this trimester?" The doctor asked as she began to skim a T-shaped wand over Jennie's stomach. The machine made noise but nothing that sounded like a heartbeat. Just a sort of echoey white noise.

The doctor looked unconcerned but Chad was holding his

breath. He leaned forward, listening intently, but hearing nothing close to a heartbeat. He was suddenly more afraid than ever that something was wrong.

Please, no. Please don't let anything be wrong.

"A few pounds," said Jennie. "I've been throwing up so much."

As she and the doctor talked, Chad wondered how they could remain so calm. He clenched his hands into fists and fought the rising panic as his heart slammed around in his chest.

Where is the heartbeat? They should have heard it by now, right?

In reality, he had no idea if the doctor should have been able to find the heartbeat more quickly or not. And, not knowing, not being in control of things, left him feeling more frightened than he was comfortable with. How would he make it through six more months of this?

"That's all right. Many women either don't gain any weight or even lose a few pounds in the first trimester. As long as it doesn't keep up, it's okay. We'll want to see you start to gain a little as you get into your second trimester."

Chad sat upright as he heard the quick flutters of a heartbeat. It sounded too fast. It made him think of a bird not a baby.

Is it supposed to sound that fast?

He eyed the doctor as his mind flipped through the pages of the book he'd been reading, but he couldn't remember reading anything about the baby's heart rate.

He caught Jennie's eyes and she smiled at him, making him melt. For a split second, he was able to pretend that she loved him as much as he loved her. That she wanted this baby to be his. That she was happy to be sharing this moment with him.

The doctor's voice cut in. "There's your baby," she smiled at them.

"Is the heartbeat too fast? That sounds really fast," he said.

"No, not at all. That's exactly what we want to hear."

All too soon, the doctor pulled away the machine and wiped Jennie's stomach, then helped her sit up on the table.

"All right. I'm going to give you a prescription for some anti-nausea meds. You still might not feel very hungry for a lot of foods. Dad," said Dr. Breckman, turning to Chad, "try foods that are similar in texture to what she's been keeping down. See if she can handle scrambled eggs, yogurt, maybe something like banana bread or pumpkin bread instead of pastries. Some pregnant women find they can stomach those little pouches of pureed baby food. They have mixtures of fruits and veggies and a pregnant woman can suck down one of those every few hours instead of eating a big meal. That can be one of the best ways for an expecting mom to get nutrients right now."

Chad was typing the list on his phone. Somewhere in the back of his mind, he knew he'd just crossed the line into crazed-father mode instead of his typical calm but he didn't give a rat's ass. He'd get more food into Jen if it killed him.

After they left the doctor's office, he pulled into the grocery store lot and left Jennie waiting in the truck. She looked worn out even from their short trip to the doctor. He dropped the prescription at the pharmacy desk and went to collect the list of foods the doctor had suggested. When he got back to the truck, he got one of those are-you-freaking-kidding-me looks from Jennie as she surveyed the six bags of groceries he piled on the back seat.

"Wow," Jennie said. "Just, wow."

He grinned at her. So, he might have overdone the groceries a bit. They probably wouldn't go through three cartons of eggs and six flavors of yogurt and forty little single-serve packets of baby food very quickly.

She laughed at him and shook her head but he didn't care. He'd heard his baby's heartbeat today. It was the most incredible feeling in the world and he damn well wasn't going to let his baby be underfed.

CHAPTER 29

*T*he baby food packets ended up being the saving grace for Jennie. She could stomach those more easily than anything else. Chad had to eat all three-dozen eggs by himself, but he didn't seem to mind. He was much happier since the doctor's visit.

And that happiness grounded her in some way.

Jennie sat on one of the rockers on the front porch watching the sun glitter on the lake. Over the past week, she'd regained a lot of her strength. The prescription the doctor had written was a godsend.

She could eat baby food and pudding and yogurt with no issues. As long as she didn't get too close to any of the food Chad was eating, she was fine. Sometimes, if she smelled his food, she'd still turn green, but even so, the worst of it seemed to be over.

As she entered her eleventh week of pregnancy, she was finally excited about the idea of a baby growing inside her. The idea that she would have this little tiny infant to hold in her arms soon.

Now if only all of the other stuff would go away. The threat from Rick Bandon. The stress of having to get up on a stand and testify against dangerous men who might hurt her or her child. The never-ending desire that thrummed through her body whenever she looked at Chad. Whenever he spoke. Whenever he was close enough for her to smell or to reach out and touch.

Which of course, she couldn't ever do again. Jennie fell asleep in the chair thinking about the feel of Chad's taut muscles under her fingers. The memory of his body above hers. The pleasure he'd brought that chased away her memories of Kyle—if only temporarily.

She wasn't sure how much time passed when her eyes fluttered open. In front of her, down by the edge of the water, she could see Chad. He stripped off his shirt as he did after every morning run. She was instantly warm all over, and a small buzz of electricity raced through her veins at the sight of his defined and tanned muscles.

Jennie felt her breath hitch, then come in short pants. Her chest rose and lowered quickly as she watched him walk into the lake to cool off. If only she could cool her response to him as easily. Instead, she waited restlessly while he swam. Then the warmth that had been running through her body pooled between her legs as he walked out of the water, dripping.

She didn't mean to stare, but she couldn't bring herself to tear her eyes off him. As he wiped his face on his T-shirt, he glanced up at her and met her eyes. She groaned, knowing he'd be able to see the unconcealed lust in her eyes.

She hadn't intended to let him know how much she wanted him. How much being locked in this cabin with him day after day had her burning with hunger.

Chad's eyes heated and his step faltered for a brief second. She looked away, swallowing to try to hide the emotions creeping up on her. She hated feeling this way. Hated needing him so much. Maybe if she kept her eyes averted, he would walk past her into the house to take his shower as he always did after his run and swim.

But, even as Jennie thought it, she knew a big part of her didn't want that. Part of her wanted him to satisfy this hunger, this craving for him that never went away. That only seemed to grow stronger each day.

Jennie felt, rather than heard, Chad stop next to her. He knelt down and she turned to look, shocked by the burning in his eyes, the intensity of the need that mirrored her own. Once again, he held her captive. She was utterly unable to break the fierce connection that burned between them. Her breath began to come too quickly and she wondered if he could see the intensity of her body's reaction to him.

She felt naked, open to him, knowing he could read everything in her eyes. Including the shock that registered when he reached up and pulled the straps of her sundress and bra down over her shoulders. She knew he caught the sharp intake of breath when his fingers slipped into the cups of her dress and bra, lowering them to expose breasts already peaked with desire for him. So sensitive, she could swear he'd be able to make her come focusing only on her breasts.

He didn't speak as he lowered his lips to savor first one tight nipple and then the other. He didn't say anything when she sucked in her breath, the feel of his mouth on her breast, instantly making her body thrum with heightened arousal, with growing need.

His eyes continued to watch her, to hold her in place, while his tongue traveled to the soft skin of the slopes of her cleavage. Skin that was so sensitive now, Jennie instantly felt the telltale build of orgasm coiling low in her belly.

She heard a whimpering moan and knew it was her own. She wanted his lips on hers. Wanted to wrap her limbs around him as he entered her, but he didn't give that to her.

He lowered himself, nestling between her legs as he lifted the skirt of her dress. Jennie's body was on fire, every touch of his hands and his mouth driving her into a frenzy of sensation. At his urging, she lifted her hips while he slid her panties down.

He used his shoulders to spread her thighs wide. His mouth was hot and wet and warm and she squirmed, raising her hips greedily in response as moan after moan left her lips. It felt completely right and completely wrong, all at once.

With gentle, persistent pressure, Chad brought Jennie to a shuddering orgasm. He drew it out with dizzying perfection, leaving her limp and stunned. Then, without a word, he covered her with her dress and walked into the house.

She sat there, stunned into silence, and tried to figure out if that had really happened or if she'd just let her imagination run away with her. If she'd wanted it so bad, she'd finally let herself believe the fantasy. If she'd wake up any minute to find it had only been a dream.

CHAPTER 30

*E*had seemed to know when Jennie's body was coiled so tight with need she thought she would snap. He'd walk up behind her when she was washing dishes and begin the slow burn she craved with every part of her being.

He'd kiss her neck, letting his tongue trace a path across spots she never knew could feel so good. He'd wrap his arms around her body, tweaking her nipples and slipping his hand into her panties to find her wet and slick.

Her body responded so quickly and intensely to his hands. He brought her to orgasm so easily that it shocked and embarrassed Jennie.

One morning, she woke to his kisses on her breasts. Again, he gave her needs priority, biting and nipping, licking and laving as she fell apart in his arms. But, she couldn't help but notice, he never kissed her on the mouth. He never made love to her or held her.

And, when she tried to turn around, to wrap her arms around him or to touch him, he held her in place. As soon as she had an orgasm, he vanished in a heartbeat, leaving her confused and alone.

She knew she should stop him, but when he wasn't touching

her, her body's demand for his touch was so great she thought it would break her. She was edgy with want when his hands weren't on her. And the minute the contact began, she was weak with the overwhelming swamp of desire and arousal, with the aching pleasure he brought. She could no more refuse his touch than she could cut off her own arm.

But, now a new ache was beginning. Jennie was desperate for the tender way he'd kissed her when they made love in Florida. She wanted the connection their lovemaking had brought. Her arms tingled with the need to reach out for him. Jennie cried into her pillow at night, begging her heart to let her go. To let her fall for this man who loved her and sacrificed over and over for her.

But her heart wouldn't free her. It still belonged to Kyle, and Kyle alone.

And as time went on, Jennie felt Chad slipping further and further away from her. He closed himself off to her more and more. His eyes became cold and shuttered when he looked at her. She saw walls going up between them that she was powerless to scale.

And, she couldn't blame him one bit. She was hurting him. Only taking, never giving. She knew it. She knew what was happening between them was only causing him further pain and heartache. And that ripped at Jennie's heart. Some days, she wanted to leave. To put space between them instead of living in this limbo that held them both captive.

Chad knocked and opened the door, drawing Jennie out of her thoughts. He held one of the disposable phones in his hand. Her heart skipped as she hoped for news from home. Maybe even news that meant she was safe and they could return.

"Jack called. Agent Burke is pushing for you to make a statement. Jack doesn't know how long he can hold him off, so we need to begin to prepare for that. We may have to make a short trip home to appease them and then slip you out of there again."

Jennie nodded at him, frightened at the idea of going home to make a statement, but excited at the possibility of getting to see her friends. Of being able to talk to her mom.

Chad held the phone out to her. "Kelly wants to talk to you. She's on a burner phone, too, so take as long as you need."

He shut the door with a quiet snick and Jennie grasped the phone like a lifeline. She couldn't believe how much she missed her friends, her life. The need to talk to her girlfriends, just to have them listen to her and tell her things would be all right was overwhelming.

"Kelly? Oh, my God, I can't believe it's you. I miss you guys so much. Tell me about Maddy. How is she? Is she growing? How big is she?"

Kelly laughed and filled Jennie in on life in Connecticut and gave her updates on Maddy, who she said was "growing more beautiful by the day."

Before Jennie knew it, she was spilling out the truth. She told Kelly what happened with Chad in Florida, about the baby, everything. All of the mixed-up feelings that filled her head and her heart every day.

She needed to have her best friend know the truth, know everything that was going on, even if they couldn't talk every day like they used to. She felt like she wasn't herself any longer and she knew Kelly would understand that.

But, Kelly was unusually quiet after Jennie stopped talking, and an uneasy feeling settled over her.

"Kelly? Are you still there?" Kelly should be reassuring her that everything would be okay, shouldn't she?

"Oh God, Jennie."

Jennie could hear in her friend's voice that she was crying and she didn't understand why.

"Jennie, I have to tell you something. I'm so, so sorry. We didn't mean for any of this to happen," Kelly said, her voice thick with tears.

Dread crept over her and Jennie wanted to hang up. She

didn't want Kelly to keep going. Didn't want to know what Kelly meant by that. Because whatever Kelly was about to tell her couldn't be good.

And Jenny could tell it would change things forever. Change things in ways that couldn't be undone.

"What are you talking about?" Jennie asked, not at all sure she wanted to hear the answer, but not able to hang up without knowing.

"When Jack sent you to the resort, he sent you and Chad together as honeymooners on purpose. He and Andrew thought it would nudge you and Chad to see if there was something real between you or not. I... Oh, God, Jennie. I'm so sorry. I knew and I let them do it."

Jennie felt cold. She didn't even know what to say. *How could Kelly do this? How could this happen?*

"Jennie, please, say something. Just talk to me."

Jennie's voice sounded foreign to her when she answered. "What do you want me to say, Kelly? I trusted you. I thought you were my friend and I trusted you with the truth about Kyle."

Suddenly Jennie was screaming and she didn't care. She didn't stop when Chad came in the room or when she heard Kelly sobbing on the other end of the phone. Something inside of her just broke and there wasn't any stopping the anger and rage that came out.

"How could you do this to me? You knew how I felt about Kyle! You knew I didn't want this! Why would you think it was okay to play with my life this way? I'm pregnant now, Kelly. My, God! What have you done?" Jennie threw the phone at the wall, where it broke, falling to the floor and cutting the call off.

The room was quiet for a minute as understanding dawned on Jennie. She looked up, horrified. Chad must have known. When she met his gaze, it was clear. The guilt was etched on his face.

"Oh, God. You didn't. Please, please tell me you didn't know about this," she said, closing her eyes and shaking her head against the truth.

"I didn't know, Jennie. I suspected but I didn't know for sure." He was quiet and calm. Just like he always was. Steadfast in the face of anything, it seemed. *Anything.* Just as calm as he always was.

But this was her life. Something in Jennie snapped.

"When, Chad? When did you suspect?" She spat out. She wanted to grab him and shake him.

He didn't answer for a few beats.

"In Jack's office. When he told us he was sending us," he said, just as quiet as ever.

"How could you know and not tell me? Why didn't you stop them? What's wrong with you?" Jennie was screaming again and on some level, she knew she should try to get herself under control but she couldn't. It was as if her whole fucked-up, crazy life was coming to a head.

Before the Florida assignment she had finally felt the first glimmer of happiness since Kyle's death—and now it was all lost. All at the hands of the people she'd thought were her friends. She'd been set up. She felt tears fall as her lip trembled and she bit down hard to stop it. She couldn't believe what she was hearing.

"I won't regret the baby, Jennie. I'm sorry for everything else that's happening, but I won't regret our baby." Chad's voice was calm and he turned to walk away. Any control Jennie had left slipped away at his cool, collected response. So measured. So in control.

She chased after him, following him through the living room and out onto the porch. She pounded small fists on his back before he stalked off the steps and whipped around to face her. He stood in the dry grass in front of the porch watching her with stormy eyes.

"Do you even feel anything, Chad? Will you for once stop

walking around, all in control and fucking calm? Do you have any idea what you all have done? I lost everything, Chad. *Everything,* when Kyle died. I lost myself."

She couldn't stop. Something in her broke and she couldn't stop. "I had finally begun to build a new life with new friends, with people I thought cared about me. I started to let myself be just a little bit happy again. Was it too much to ask? Did I ask for too much by just wanting to have a little bit of a life again?" She scarcely took a breath, pouring all her anger into her words. "Now, it's all screwed up again and you walk around here like you don't feel anything about what's happened."

For only the second time since she'd known him, she saw the flash of anger on his face, so fierce her breath caught in her throat and she took an involuntary step back, away from him. She knew he would never hurt her on purpose, but the anger rolling off him was palpable. It seemed to force her backwards as if it had a life of its own, a power of its own.

"Not feel anything, Jennie? Are you fucking kidding me? I walk around here every day and I ache every fucking minute I'm with you. I'm so twisted up with loving you and hating you, I can't breathe. I can't keep my hands off you, but I can't let myself kiss you because I might lose myself in you. I can't make love to you because I'm afraid you'll pretend I'm him. That you'll close your eyes and pretend it's Kyle inside you. I know you want his arms around you, not mine. I know you want it to be his baby inside you, not mine. And I know you can't love me back, no matter what I do, because you're still so in love with your husband, you can't even begin to see me."

He didn't stop and she didn't try to stop him. She was frozen in place as she watched Chad come undone. As she watched and realized his heartache was as big as hers.

"And every day, I have to sit here and wonder how I'll be a part of my baby's life. I wonder if you'll let me be in the delivery room, if you'll let me help you name the baby. I wonder how much money I'd have to offer the people who live across the street from you to buy their house, just so I can see my child grow up. If you'll let me—" Chad stopped as if he'd run out of steam.

They stood in uneasy silence for a long time before he spoke again. He sounded worn out and bitter and angry, mirroring Jennie's chaos of emotions.

"Am I feeling anything? Yeah. I'm feeling some fucking shit, Jen." He turned and walked through the trees, leaving her on the porch of the cabin, ripped open. Feeling everything in her life was broken.

And, worse than the fact that she had no idea how to fix things, was the fact that she had no idea if she even wanted to.

CHAPTER 31

C had slowed to a walk. He didn't know how many miles he'd run. Longer than his typical morning run. He shouldn't have left Jennie alone at the cabin so long, but he knew he couldn't go back there right now. He felt more mixed up than ever.

It was time to take Jennie home. He needed to get her back to New Haven. Get her testimony on record before they both got arrested for impeding a federal investigation. Then he'd figure out a way to keep her safe without the sheer and utter torture of living in a small, isolated cabin with her.

He didn't know if his mom had been right about him wanting to be unhappy or not. Maybe he had done this to himself subconsciously. And if he had, he was sorry he'd dragged Jennie into it. She didn't deserve to be paying the price for his fucked-up head.

Chad knew it was time to move on. He'd love his baby and he'd find a way to raise it with Jennie, as friends, but he needed to find a way to stop loving her.

Being here with her, and yet not with her, made him realize how important it was that he move on and build a life, create a family with someone who could love him back and make him happy.

He knew deep down his mother was right about one thing. He did feel guilty for coming home from the war. He'd left so many friends behind. Good people who already had families of their own waiting for them to come back.

And for reasons Chad couldn't understand, he got to come home and many of them didn't. And, yeah, he'd always hated that. Always wished he could have brought all of them back with him. So, yeah, maybe on some level, he'd though he shouldn't get to have what they could never come back to: love, a family.

But he couldn't go on like this. And he couldn't wish to trade places with them because he wouldn't wish that pain on his mom or Jack or his friends. Taking a deep breath, Chad bent and put his hands on his knees and closed his eyes.

It's time.

And as he took cleansing breath after cleansing breath, he let it all go. All the guilt and anger and feeling that maybe he was somehow undeserving of the life he had. The life that had been spared. And, he let his guilt over Jennie go as well.

He wouldn't regret loving her even though he had to face the fact that she might never love him back. Her heart had been buried with her husband. But, maybe their baby would bring her some happiness, and for that, Chad would be grateful.

Taking one last deep breath, he turned back toward the cabin. It was time to take Jennie home.

They left the cabin three days later. Chad didn't tell anyone they were coming. The less anyone knew about their whereabouts, the better. He still had plenty of cash stashed away so there was no need to use credit cards or anything that could be traced.

They planned to go to Jennie's parents' house first to see them, then spend no more than a day or two getting Jennie's testimony taken care of before heading back to the cabin. From there, he'd figure out their next step.

He wasn't thrilled with this plan, but Jennie was adamant about going to her parents' house. And, she'd made a few good points in her argument. No one was expecting them. They wouldn't call Burke until they arrived. They wouldn't let anyone else know their location.

Even Chad had to admit, it was highly unlikely that Rick Bandon would be sitting on her parents' house an hour away from where she lived. If anything, Bandon would be watching Jennie's house or maybe Chad's condo in New Haven.

So, in the end, she won. Meanwhile, Chad was brainstorming a longer-term way to keep her safe, one that didn't require them to live in such close confines. He needed to find a way to step back and let the feelings he had for her fade away.

They'd fallen back into an uneasy truce, of sorts, but they didn't talk much and things were strained. He could see dark circles forming under Jennie's eyes again and knew she wasn't sleeping well.

He pulled off the highway a half hour from Jennie's parents' house. He dug out a burner phone they hadn't used yet and pulled a sheet of phone numbers from his wallet. He punched in one of the phone numbers and handed the phone to Jennie after placing it on speaker.

"Don't tell your parents where we are and don't let on that we're coming. Tell them we're hopping from one hotel to another," he said as the phone rang.

She nodded.

"Jennie? Is that you?" Her mother sounded about like you'd expect. Desperate for news. Desperate to hear her daughter's voice.

"Yeah, Mom, it's me. Chad's on the line, too."

"Hi, Chad, honey. How are you guys?"

Chad would have smiled at the way Jennie's mom greeted him

as if he were just as important to her as Jennie was, but he needed to stay focused on getting Jennie in and out quickly.

"We're great, Mom. We're staying in hotels right now, but it's not too bad," Jennie said.

"We wanted to check in and see if you've seen anything unusual there. Has anyone been around that shouldn't be? Anyone who seems out of place?" Chad asked.

"No," Jennie's mom said, "nothing unusual."

"How about any houses for lease or rent on your block. Or any houses that are empty for renovations or anything like that?" Chad asked.

Jennie's mother was quiet, as if she were thinking, before answering, "No."

"Have you seen any workmen or a new mail carrier on your route? Telephone repair? Construction nearby?"

"No," came the answer, the tension in her voice clear.

Chad nodded at Jennie and pulled off the road as she finished her conversation with her mom. They talked for a few minutes before ending the call quite close to her parents' house.

When they pulled into the driveway in the early evening, he took out a new cell phone and texted Agent Burke to arrange for Burke to take Jennie's statement the following day.

He texted her parents' address and told Burke to have an agent come there for the statement. He said he would keep her there for twenty-four hours only before they moved on so if Burke wanted his statement, he needed to get there in that time-frame. Chad wanted to control things as much as possible.

Jack would have lawyers on standby if Burke tried to force Chad's hand and keep Jennie in the area.

Jennie's parents came out of the house and enveloped her in tears and hugs. He could see their disappointment when she told them the visit would only be for a day and then she and Chad would go back into hiding. They tried to be upbeat about it, but the strain of the situation was clear in the tightness of their features.

Chad shook hands with Jennie's father, Phil, and hugged her mother, Barb. He had met them once before at Kelly and Jack's wedding and knew they were the type of people that immediately welcomed friends as if they were family.

"We're going over to the Evans' house for a barbeque in a few minutes. They'll be thrilled to see you," said Jennie's mom.

It struck Chad then that Jennie's last name—Evans—was her married name. He'd never really thought about it before, but of course she still went by it.

The front door of the house on the left opened then and Chad assumed the man and woman drawing Jennie into more hugs were Kyle's parents. He nodded politely when they were introduced as Annie and Brian Evans.

When they all settled into the Evans' backyard, drinks in hand, burgers on the grill, Chad could almost pretend things were normal. But they weren't.

He saw the second when Jennie's mother noticed the changes in her daughter's body and turned an uneasy look toward Chad. Jennie wasn't really showing yet, but maybe mothers somehow know these things about their daughters. Her waist was ever so slightly thicker than it had been and her breasts were bigger, but you couldn't tell very easily with the shirt she had on.

Chad ducked his head against her mother's look. Jennie would have to be the one to tell her this news. It wasn't his place.

They gathered inside, in a casual dining room, for dinner. When the plates had been filled with burgers, coleslaw, potato salad, and corn, Chad saw Jennie fight back nausea as she eyed her plate.

He knew perfectly well she couldn't eat this food. He didn't know how she planned to fake it. He got up and went to his duffle bag by the door and returned with two baby food pouches. He

166 | LORI RYAN

handed them to Jennie without a word, despite the four questioning gazes that jumped between him and Jennie.

He knew he wasn't being very subtle about her inability to eat real food, but he wasn't in the mood for games. She needed to tell her parents the truth. Besides, a few more minutes trying to pretend she could eat that food and she'd be running to the bathroom. Trying to slip her the food pouches unseen somehow would just be futile.

"Thank you," Jennie murmured and opened one pouch to eat it. Chad removed her plate, putting it aside so the smell of the burger wouldn't make her sick. The medicine the doctor had given her helped a lot, but Jennie was still overly sensitive to strong smells.

"All right," Jennie's mother said, tossing her napkin on the table and standing up. "What's going on, Jennie? Chad?"

"You need to tell them. Jennie. Your mom's already guessed," Chad said quietly.

"What? No, she hasn't!" Jennie shook her head, her eyes wide, as if she were still trying to will everything away.

"Jennie, you're either sick or you're pregnant, but you're scaring the wits out of me. Tell me which one it is," Jennie's mother said. Kyle's mother didn't look surprised but the men sure did.

They dropped their forks and gaped.

It must be a mother thing. Mothers seemed to have radar.

Jennie looked up into the faces of her parents and her in-laws. Faces that showed nothing but love and worry for the woman sitting in front of them. And, then she bolted.

CHAPTER 32

This can't be happening. It just can't be happening.
Jennie hadn't planned on telling her parents about the baby on this trip, and she certainly hadn't planned to tell them in front of Kyle's parents. She wasn't showing yet so she hadn't even thought she'd need to face this so soon. She thought she had time.

She paced in the living room as Zeke circled around her, whining. Chad came quietly into the room and sat on the couch —ready and waiting as if on standby until she needed him.

She realized he'd always be there for her. Always be ready to help her, to save her, when she needed him.

Why he still cared about her, she couldn't figure out. She'd caused him so much pain. After all the horrible things she'd said to him, he still sat ready and willing to help her.

It wasn't long before the others followed him, waiting for her to explain.

"Jennie, please tell me you're not sick. Please." Her mother spoke quietly, but the panic in her voice was evident.

"I'm sorry, Mom. I'm not sick." Jennie swiped at tears and wrapped her arms around herself, holding tight.

She still hadn't admitted to being pregnant, but based on her answer it was now clear to everyone in the room.

Jennie's dad met Chad's gaze. He didn't sound angry when he spoke, which surprised Jennie. "Do you love her, Chad?"

Chad looked straight at her father when he answered. "Very much, but unfortunately, that's not relevant here."

Jennie felt her breath coming in shallow gasps and she thought she might pass out. A small part of her realized she was probably hyperventilating but she didn't know what to do about that.

She didn't know how to stop what was happening. She wanted it all to just stop. Her arms shook as she tried to will away the events unfolding before her.

It was Kyle's mom who spoke next. Jennie had always loved her as much as she loved her own mother. It hurt to have both women looking at her now. She wanted to hide, to crawl away and curl up, instead of facing this.

"Jennie, honey, I know you loved Kyle. I know how hard it was for you to lose him. But, it's time, honey. It's time for you to let him go. It's time to let yourself be happy again."

Don't they understand? Don't they get it? She couldn't be happy. Wouldn't be happy in another man's arms. They didn't understand what she had done. They didn't know she was the reason their son died.

Tears streamed, unencumbered, down Jennie's face as she faced the people who loved her. Would they still love her if they knew the truth?

"Jennie—" Kyle's dad took an almost imperceptible step forward and seemed to want to reach for her, but didn't. "Honey, she's right. Kyle wouldn't want to see you like this. He wouldn't want you to give up on having a life, on finding love again, just because he's gone."

She heard the murmured agreements by those around her, but she knew the truth. She knew what they didn't know. What no one could know.

The words were wrenched from her soul, but it was time to tell them. "I can't. I... You don't know. I'm the reason he died. I killed Kyle."

The words came pouring out in a torrent that Jennie couldn't control, couldn't check in any way.

"I told him to wait. Kyle was sick and getting so many headaches. He was tired all the time, but he had just started his new job. When we graduated from school, Kyle started it right away but I didn't have a job yet. Money was so tight and his health insurance wouldn't kick in until he'd been at his job for ninety days."

Jennie doubled over feeling like the emotion of telling them would cut her in two, but Chad's arms came around her, catching her.

He lifted her up and carried her to the couch, where he cradled her in his arms and held her tight while she continued to talk through the tears.

"When he was in the hospital, I asked the doctor, 'If we had found it earlier, would that have made a difference?' He said every day, every week, with cancer treatment makes a difference. Because of me, Kyle waited three months before seeing a doctor. Three months could have saved him. He could be here with us instead of gone if I hadn't been so selfish."

As Jennie leaned into Chad and cried, he shushed her, and rocked her, surrounded by Kyle's parents and her parents.

She looked up at them and couldn't understand why they all still looked at her with love in their eyes. With understanding and concern instead of hatred. Why weren't they looking at her with disgust after what she just told them? Didn't they understand?

Kyle's mom leaned close and took Jennie's hand in hers. "Jennie, you didn't kill Kyle. You listen to me, sweetheart. That doctor had no right to tell you that. No right at all, sweetheart. You and Kyle were so young when you married. You'd have no reason to think he was so sick. None of us did. I brought him chicken soup, for heaven's sake, Jennie. I didn't make him go to a doctor. I made him soup."

Jennie's breath was ragged and her throat hurt from trying to choke in air around the sobs. Her chest hitched uncontrollably with every inhale as she tried to process what was said.

And through it all, Chad held on tight to her, rocking her until she wore herself out and the flow of tears began to slow.

As she caught her breath, Kyle's father spoke so quietly she almost couldn't hear him at first.

"Kyle knew, Jennie," he said.

"What?" Her head snapped up and it sounded as if everyone in the room was holding their breath. She could tell by the look on their faces, no one else had known this secret either.

"He told me. About a week before he died. He told me he had gone to a clinic without telling you. He used a fake name so it wouldn't be on his work medical record as a preexisting condition. They told him he needed to start treatment right away, but he didn't want to strap you with that burden financially. By that time, it was only a matter of about five more weeks before his insurance kicked in, so he waited. He made a choice, Jennie. And, it wasn't that choice that killed him and it wasn't you that killed him. It was cancer that killed Kyle. It wasn't fair and it wasn't right for him or for you to have to go through that, but that doesn't make it your fault, Jennie.

She stared in shock as she tried to process what he'd just said. As she tried to absorb the fact that maybe, just maybe, she'd held onto a guilt she shouldn't have had to bear all these years. For four years, she'd held on.

She'd punished herself, never allowing her heart to move on. And, now, in the span of only minutes, she'd been told by people she loved and believed, that she didn't have to. That it was all right to finally let it all go.

CHAPTER 33

*D*inner forgotten, they all settled in the living room as Chad held Jennie in his arms. She had worn herself out. She lay limp against him, having finally succumbed to sleep.

He suspected she hadn't been sleeping well since they had their fight at the cabin. He leaned back against the couch, shifting sideways so he could let her stretch out a bit and sleep.

Her parents and in-laws surrounded them, as if unable to pull themselves away. Her father started talking first, and initially, Chad wished they wouldn't tell him about Kyle. But, after a minute, he realized they weren't.

They were really telling him about Jennie because Kyle was as much a part of Jennie as they all were. To really know Jennie, Chad had to know Kyle, too. He had to know the whole story.

"She used to follow him around when he was twelve. She thought he hung the moon and the stars, but he thought she had cooties at that age," Jennie's dad said, laughing at the memory.

Chad could picture Jennie then. He pictured a young version of the happier Jennie he used to know, not the woman she had been in the last few months.

"She would do things to get his attention like hide his football or put itching powder down the back of his shorts," said Kyle's mom.

"Oh, God. I remember that! The things she put that poor boy through," said Jennie's mom shaking her head.

They began to tell stories about Jennie and Kyle. About the year Kyle finally noticed girls in general, and Jennie in particular. About their junior prom and their senior prom.

About Kyle saving up to buy Jennie a promise ring and the time they caught Kyle climbing the trellis to get to Jennie's room at night.

About how Kyle proposed to Jennie at the family celebration of Kyle's college graduation and how she cried when he got down on one knee.

They talked late into the night as Jennie slept. Chad thought he would feel jealous, hearing about her perfect relationship with the man he couldn't begin to compete with. But he didn't.

He liked hearing about how happy Jennie had been. He wanted that back for her. It hurt like hell that he couldn't give her that happiness, but if he couldn't give it to her, he wanted her to find it any way she could.

Eventually, the stories of Kyle and Jennie stopped and the group sat quietly for a bit even though it was well past midnight. It was as though none of them could stand to leave Jennie for the short time she'd be home.

They had turned out the lights and had only a small lamp on as they talked. At some point they'd eaten cold burgers, bringing the plates in from the dining room to eat picnic style in the living room.

"What do you think you want it to be, Chad? A boy or a girl?" Jennie's dad grinned as he asked the question.

"Oh, it can't be a girl," Chad said with an equally big grin that told them he really didn't care if it was a boy or a girl. "Then two women will have me wrapped around their little fingers," he said with mock fear in his voice. "I can't have that."

As they laughed, Chad heard a car creep to a halt outside Jennie's parents' house next door. He went immediately on alert just as Zeke stood and growled, low and in his throat. It wasn't a loud bark. It was an almost silent warning.

The headlights on the car were cut before it even finished pulling to the curb and whoever was in it didn't exit right away.

Chad sat Jennie up, placing a finger to his lips to indicate to the group to be quiet.

"Jen," he shook her a little. "Jen, did you tell anyone we were here? Text or call anyone?"

She looked at him with confusion in her gaze but shook her head, no.

Chad looked up at the couples sitting around him. "Have you called anyone since we arrived?"

He had a bad feeling about this. And he trusted his gut. It had kept him alive in a lot of tough situations.

All four of them shook their heads.

Chad left Jennie on the couch and motioned to everyone to stay put. He slipped his Glock out of his duffel and held it by his right leg as he went to the window to watch Jennie's house.

Two men exited the car. He didn't recognize them, but their dark clothing furthered the feeling of unease coming over him. As he watched, they crept toward the house carrying large containers. It took only seconds for Chad to recognize they had containers of gasoline.

He grabbed his phone and tossed it to Jennie's dad. "They're setting your house on fire. Call 911. Tell them what I look like and what I'm wearing. Stay inside until I get back," he said as he turned toward the back of the house.

He heard Jennie cry out behind him, but he had to leave her. He needed to find out who the men next door were and how they'd tracked them down. Once the police arrived, he wouldn't have a shot at any of that.

He crossed through the dining room, grabbing one of the

cloth napkins from the table and tying it around his mouth and nose, cowboy style. He went into the kitchen, then slipped out into the yard.

He moved silently as he took in the location of the men next door. He stopped and listened, focusing only on the sounds around him. He could hear one man at the front of the house and one at the back. And neither was expecting him.

Chad hoped he could get to them before one of them lit a match. The smell of gasoline was overpowering, even with his impromptu mask, as he got closer to the house. Using a gun was out of the question with so much accelerant around.

It was clear that the men weren't professionals and had no clue what they were doing. Surrounding the house with gasoline wasn't a very effective way of burning it down. They needed to be working from the inside out. Not to mention, the men hadn't even checked to be sure Jennie was inside the house before they started.

Whoever had sent these guys hadn't taken the time to find someone who knew what they were doing. They were either acting hastily or were acting on someone else's plan, with little thought as to how to execute it.

Chad moved into position behind the man at the back of the house. The guy was tall but looked to be fairly out of shape, his gut hanging over the top of his pants.

Chad moved quickly, grabbing him in a carotid hold designed to cut the blood supply to the man's brain. It was a very quick way to render someone unconscious, and usually worked faster than a choke hold. He felt the man go limp in his arms.

With no cuffs or zip ties to secure the first arsonist, he'd have to hope he was able to take out the second man before the first one came to. He lowered him to the ground and listened for his accomplice.

The sound of trampling through the bushes told Chad the second man was heading around the side of the house toward him. Chad ducked into the shadows against the side of the house and waited.

"Barry," came the man's voice in a whisper. "Barry? Where the hell are you?"

Chad stepped from the shadows, leading with his fist. The second man was in better shape than the first. It wasn't easy to take a dead-on hit from Chad like that and still be standing, but he came back at Chad with a right cross and a series of jabs.

Chad deflected the man's blows, waiting for an opening. When one came, he exploded, shoving the man back against the house with a series of shots. When his adversary's back hit the house, Chad cut off his air supply with a forearm across the neck.

"Who sent you?" Chad growled.

The man clawed at his arm with ineffective hands, his eyes bulging as he fought for breath.

Chad eased up a fraction, allowing the man a small amount of air as he asked again, "Who. Sent. You." His tone was deadly and fierce because he needed to extract any information he could, quickly. Once the police came, there wouldn't be a chance for any more of Chad's style of questioning.

The man shook his head and Chad pressed in once again, cutting off the assailant's air supply. Hearing sirens, he knew his time was up.

Whoever this guy was, he wasn't talking easily. Chad yanked the arsonist around and gripped both his arms in a hold behind the man's back. He shoved him ahead of him to meet the police as his mind processed the implications of this attack.

Only one person knew he and Jennie were back in town and where they were. He hadn't even called Jack and Kelly or his mother to tell them they were coming.

Nope. There was only one person other than the people sitting in the Evans' living room who knew where he and Jennie were. Agent Burke.

~

As the police car pulled away from the house, Chad turned to Jennie's parents.

"Pack a bag quickly. We need to get out of here before Bandon finds out they failed and sends someone else. Meet back out here in five minutes. Tops."

They didn't argue. Chad's tone hadn't left much room for that and they loved Jennie as much as he did. They wanted her safe as much as Chad.

He turned to Kyle's parents next. "I doubt they know about you, so you should be safe here, but if you'd rather go stay at a hotel with Jennie's parents, I'm happy to pay for it. We can get you guys a suite and call it a vacation," he said, smiling.

Most people weren't used to dealing with arson attempts in the middle of the night. A little levity couldn't hurt.

Chad didn't miss the look Annie gave her husband. She was frightened. Her hands griped his arm and her husband seemed to pick up on it right away.

"A vacation sounds good right about now," Brian Evans said. "Where will you and Jennie be going?"

"We've got to go see one of my friends with the FBI. If Agent Burke leaked Jennie's location, we need to bring him and Rick Bandon in quickly."

Kyle's father nodded and walked toward the house with his wife to pack their things. Chad waited on the front lawn, eyes on the road, scanning in case any other unexpected visitors arrived. They were sitting ducks right now. He needed to get them out of here. Quickly.

CHAPTER 34

*A*fter getting Jennie's family set up with their new bodyguard at a hotel, Chad and Jennie drove to his condo in New Haven. It was nearly dawn, but Chad had to work out who had sent the two men to Jennie's parents' house.

After getting Jennie safely inside, he called the only person he trusted to help him take down a dirty federal agent.

Mike Hayes was a Supervisory Special Agent in the New Haven field office. Mike served in the military with a close friend of Chad's and if there were dirty federal agents in the office, Chad was sure Mike wasn't involved. Mike was clean as a whistle and as dedicated to the agency as they came.

Mike set things in motion quickly, getting in touch with Burke's supervising agent and the Assistant United States Attorney in charge of the case, Caroline Waters.

AUSA Waters would have worked closely with Burke on the case and would have as much information to help them flush out any leaks as Burke's supervisor would. She'd be able to help them figure out what they could and couldn't do quickly within the bounds of the law, and she could help push through any warrants they needed in a hurry.

Since Burke's phone belonged to the FBI, not Burke, they

didn't need to wait for a warrant to dump his phone records. With Burke back in Florida and Jennie here in Connecticut, normal procedure meant he should have called a field agent in Connecticut to take Jennie's statement here. The phone logs would easily show if he'd done that or called someone else—Rick Bandon, for example.

Chad and Mike formulated a plan. The details would stay within their small circle of Chad, Mike, AUSA Waters, and Burke's supervising agent. No one else would know the full details of what they were doing.

Burke would be given a fake meeting location and time. It would be a location that was not anywhere near Jennie. Mike would bring in a decoy posing as Jennie. Even the decoy wouldn't have the full story.

Then, they'd wait to see what Burke did. If information had been leaked, they'd have their source, and hopefully, enough leverage to lead to the location of Rick Bandon.

Chad got off the phone with Mike and looked over at the couch. Jennie was curled in a ball, fast asleep with Zeke on the floor by her feet. He scooped her up and started down the hall toward the guest room he'd put her things in earlier, cradling her small body against his. He needed to make her safe, at all costs.

Jennie snuggled deeper into Chad's arms, wrapping her arms around his neck. When he stopped at the guest room, Jennie shook her head.

"Take me to your room," she whispered.

She wanted to be with him. She had no idea where this was going, but she knew that much. She needed to be near Chad.

Somehow, things had changed in the last day. It was as if tiny slivers of light had begun to come through the gray shadows that surrounded Jennie since Kyle died.

She wasn't sure if it was the talk about Kyle's death that started to let some light in, or something else altogether. But she felt better.

Her feelings for Chad swirled in her heart and her head and she didn't know what she wanted. She only knew she didn't want to let him go. She didn't want him to leave her.

Chad set her feet on the floor of his room. Two minutes ago, Jennie had felt so tired she was sure she would fall asleep as soon as her head hit the pillow. Now, with one look, Chad set her body on fire again.

"I should let you sleep," he said in a low voice that sent shivers through her. His eyes burned with intensity and his body brushed hers, letting her know he wanted her just as much as she wanted him.

"I don't think I want you to," she answered, pressing into him, letting her breasts graze his chest, her stomach feel the hardness of his erection as it pushed into her.

Chad trailed one finger down her neck, over her collarbone, and down to the supple curve of her breast. Warmth rushed through her body, waking her instantly.

"What do you want, Jen?"

She loved it when he called her Jen. It was such a common nickname for people named Jennifer but for some reason, she'd always been Jennie to everyone. Only Chad called her Jen.

She stood on tiptoe and ran her hands up his chest, and around his neck, pulling him down to her mouth.

"You," she whispered against his lips. "This time, it's not about forgetting. And it's not about wanting to stop the pain. This time, it's about you. I want to be with you. I want to experience every moment, savor every touch, taste, and sensation."

She wanted to be present as they came together.

She unbuttoned his shirt slowly, one button at a time, loving the way his breath changed as her hands moved over him. Shorter, harsher breaths told the story of her effect on his body.

She felt the intensity of his gaze on her, bringing the heat in her to a boil as her breath began to match his with the quickening she'd come to realize would always happen at his touch.

She leaned in and pressed her lips to his chest, hearing a rumbling growl from Chad in response. Her hands traveled greedily and her mouth explored the taut lines of his muscular torso.

And then his hands were on her, and he lifted her swiftly, turning to lay her on the bed as though he couldn't wait another minute to take her.

She laughed at the thrill of making Chad's control snap, but her laughter died, replaced with a gasp as he lowered his body over hers. He framed her face with his arms and her mouth, kissing her deeply, intently. She knew what Chad had meant when he'd said he could get lost in her if they kissed. She was lost in him.

He lifted the hem of her shirt and pressed kisses to her stomach, playing lazily back and forth on the few inches of skin he'd exposed above the waistline of her pants.

Jennie felt like every nerve ending in her skin was hypersensitive somehow. Even the slightest touch sent her reeling and moaning, and wanting more. So much more.

Chad gradually pushed her shirt up, taking his time to reach the bottom slope of her breasts. He kissed and nuzzled, letting his lips trail over the lace of her bra, teasing and taunting until she thought she would scream.

Every inch of her body tingled now, as if it cried out for more from him and Jennie knew she'd be reduced to begging if he kept up this maddeningly slow pace.

His mouth was hot when it closed around one nipple as his hand teased her other breast. She couldn't believe how incredibly turned on she was and she didn't even have her clothes off yet.

He sat her up and slipped her shirt over her head. He kissed the inside of her wrist, the curve at the inside of her elbow, then her shoulder. Each kiss ratcheted Jennie's body to new heights of arousal.

He laid her back on the bed and began to remove her yoga pants, sliding them down her hips and thighs at a painfully tortuous pace.

Each inch of skin he revealed was laced with kisses or nips or soft breaths of hot air before he continued. Each inch of skin he revealed was set on fire.

When her pants landed on the chair, he sat on the edge of the bed and took one of her feet into his lap. His fingers grazed over her ankles as he slipped her sock off. One hand slid up her leg, caressing, sending her body trembling. The other hand took hold of her other foot and slipped the sock off.

Jennie watched in awe. How did he make removing her socks so incredibly sensual? And how did he have the control to do this? Her body shook with need as Chad slipped his hands beneath her bottom and lifted her hips, settling his mouth between her legs.

She knew she was already swollen, slick, and wet when his tongue touched her. He circled and swirled, teasing her, building pleasure with every second.

"Chad," Jennie whispered on a moan.

"Mmm hmm?" he murmured, his lips against her labia, driving her wild.

"I need..."

"Mmmmmm?" He murmured against her hot flesh, almost sending her flying. "What is it that you need, Jen?"

"To feel...to feel you, Chad. To feel everything."

He slid two fingers inside her in answer and she felt her muscles clench around him, pulsating and tight. He slipped them out then pressed in again, his mouth on her clitoris, sending her over the edge.

He drew out her orgasm, letting her feel every sensation,

every emotion, every sensual delight he brought upon her. She didn't think she'd ever come down from the sheer pleasure.

It felt like she was floating on a cloud as Chad's hands and mouth played over her body, sending her to heights she'd never imagined.

~

Chad called on every ounce of self-control he possessed. Just hearing Jennie say she wanted to feel instead of forget meant she wanted to be here with him, in this moment.

She wasn't trying to forget her pain or pretend she was back in Kyle's arms. She was here with Chad.

And, he would make sure he gave her everything she needed, more if he could. He'd felt a shift in her since she had told her family about the guilt she'd been carrying over Kyle's death. He still knew she didn't love him the way he loved her. But for now, knowing she wanted to be here in this moment with him was enough.

As Chad felt the orgasm race through Jennie's body, he pulled back. He watched in amazement as her face reflected what her body was feeling. She was stunning. There just weren't any words for the beauty he saw in her.

When she began to come back to him, he gently licked and teased, coming close to where she needed his touch the most, but knowing she'd be too sensitive there right now. He slowly swirled and circled around her clitoris, not touching yet.

He gradually wound her back up again as she twisted, pleading, beneath his mouth and hands. And when she was ready, he slipped his fingers into her and closed his mouth over her while she moaned and called out his name.

Chad loved the sight of Jennie naked and pulsing with need beneath him. He could watch her come apart over and over and never tire of it. He slowly lowered his head again, but kept his eyes on her face. He captured her clit with his mouth and sucked hard as she spiraled off into an orgasm again. He'd never get enough of that.

The sounds of her sweet, raspy release were mesmerizing. The way her body glistened with a thin layer of perspiration. The way she thrashed beneath him, moaning and gasping. The look of sheer joy on her face.

The way her body tightened around his fingers, swollen and wet and hot. He could do this again and again for the rest of their lives. If only she'd let him.

Chad reached into the nightstand by the bed for a condom.

He kept his eyes on hers as he came back to the bed with her. He lowered himself over her, then took her mouth with his. God, how he loved this woman.

"Jennie," he whispered, his lips still against hers.

Gently, Chad entered her, barely suppressing a groan at the feel of his hard length gripped by her. He held still for a minute, regaining control. He wanted this to last longer than the thirty seconds it was looking like it would be right then.

"I won't ever get enough of this feeling, Jen."

Her arms wrapped around his neck, her legs around his waist. He didn't break the contact with her mouth as he drew out slowly, then plunged back in. Deep, long, slow.

He didn't let himself go like he would have liked. If Jennie wasn't pregnant, he'd be driving into her hard and fast and deep over and over again until they were both spinning out of control. Instead, he moved slowly, drawing back until only the head of his erection was barely inside her before plunging equally slowly back in again.

Her soft mewls were low and pleading, driving him to insanity as his body wound closer and closer to orgasm. He broke from her mouth and lowered his head to her breast. The feel of her pebbled nipple against his tongue was decadent and sensual.

He closed his mouth around her breast as he pushed into her sweet, wet folds with one last, deep thrust.

He felt her orgasm as she tightened around him and cried out. And he followed her, finally, letting himself go. Letting himself get lost in her, knowing he wouldn't be able to turn back now. Whether she ever returned his love or not, he would love this woman for the rest of his life.

CHAPTER 35

Jennie and Chad slept through much of the day, trying to catch up on sleep they'd missed the night before. They woke in the early evening to a call from Mike.

"What's up?" Chad asked as Jennie sat up beside him in bed, one hand resting on his back.

He wrapped his arm around her, pulling her close as he listened to Mike. The thought that something might happen to Jennie now, after all they'd been though, made Chad sick. He needed to end this. He needed to find a way to keep her safe.

"There's been a delay in getting Burke's phone messages. Some kind of technical glitch, supposedly. I don't know how soon we'll get the records, but I've been in touch with Burke's supervisor. He wants us to go ahead with the meeting with Burke," Mike said.

Chad cursed under his breath. "Okay. Set it up."

"I want you to go in with a decoy. I've got an undercover agent we can pass off as Jennie, but I want you to be there to fill in any details or answer any questions she may not have answers to. I've briefed her on everything Jennie saw and heard and she'll be ready to go by the time we meet, but I want you there as backup."

Chad hesitated. If he was at the meeting, he couldn't be with Jennie. He couldn't be by her side, keeping her safe. But, he also knew they'd never be able to stop running if he didn't flush out Bandon and anyone else who was helping Bandon.

Chad's eyes caught Jennie's and he knew she couldn't keep living on the run. No one, other than him and Mike, Burke's supervisor and the attorney assigned to the case would know she was here and security in his building was tight. He decided he could leave her here safely.

Mike and Chad chose a time and location for the following day. With any luck, they'd draw Bandon out of hiding, prove Burke was guilty of leaking information —at the very least—and most likely of accepting bribes that could have the case tied up without Jennie's testimony, by the following day.

Jennie watched Chad talk on the phone and tried to make sense of the emotions swirling around in her head and her heart. This was only the second time she had slept in his arms, despite the fact that they'd lived together for a month.

The first time, in Florida, Jennie had been hiding from her feelings. Today, she still couldn't say she was completely open to her feelings for Chad, but she was a lot more open to them than she had been a few days earlier.

She was beginning to accept how much she cared for him. He'd been her friend for so long. Her support in so many ways. He protected her. He cared for her without question whenever she needed him.

But there was more than that. He made her feel special. Cherished. He made her laugh and he held her when she cried. So many men would have walked away from her a long time ago, considering what she'd put him through. She knew it would never have crossed Chad's mind to do that.

Chad hung up the phone and turned to Jennie. Before she could speak, he pulled her into his arms and kissed her slowly, deeply. Jennie felt herself relax into him. He felt so...right. But a small part of Jennie still panicked at what that might mean.

Chad pulled back. "You okay?"

Jennie nodded, forcing herself to breathe deeply. She needed to put the past behind her and let herself see where things could go with Chad. She owed herself that. More than that, she owed Chad that much.

"I'm good. Hungry," she said, patting her tummy. As if on cue, her stomach growled.

With a laugh, he stood and put his hand out to pull Jennie up with him.

If she weren't pregnant and very much in need of food, the sight of Chad without anything on would have sent her tumbling right back into bed. She would never get over the sight of him like that.

Jennie thought she could spend hours learning every inch of his body, exploring every muscle, memorizing each taut line and every scar from his days in the military.

"Keep looking at me like that and we're not getting food any time soon," Chad said, eyes ablaze as they took her in.

"Sorry, baby needs food," she answered, with one hand on her stomach again.

He dropped a kiss to her mouth then pulled on a pair of boxers and a shirt.

"Why don't you get dressed? I'll see if there's anything to eat in the kitchen. There won't be anything fresh but I might have some frozen bread I can toast to tide us over."

Jennie's repertoire of foods she could eat was still a bit limited. They walked down the hall together with Chad breaking off to turn toward the kitchen and Jennie heading into the guest room to get her clothes. She pulled on a sundress then sat staring at her purse for a few minutes. She knew what she needed to do.

She just needed a minute to build up the courage to take the next step.

She took a deep breath and went to the small zippered pocket of her purse. The envelope she withdrew was soft with age. Some of the seams were threatening to give up. It was still sealed. In all these years, she'd transferred it from purse to purse, never opening it.

Kyle had told her to open it when she was ready. She never had been.

She wasn't sure she was ready now, but she knew she had to get there. It was time for her to put the past behind her. Jennie sat on the edge of the bed for a long time before she slipped a finger under the flap, tearing along the well-worn seam. Her hands shook as she unfolded the single sheet of paper.

She laughed through her tears as she read the first sentence.

How many years did it take, Jennie? One? Two? I hope not more than that, Bugsy.

Jennie had no idea how Kyle had come up with the nickname 'Bugsy' for her, but he had. And, it had stuck.

I thought I could beat this thing, but I waited too long. I thought there was so much time, but it turns out I was wrong about that. I wanted so many more years with you.

I wanted a lifetime to make you happy. To make you laugh. To raise babies with you and see what an amazing mom you would be. I wanted all of that and I'm so sorry I couldn't give that to you. I'm so sorry.

I know it's cliché but I want you to fall in love again, Jennie. I know you. You'll resist it. You'll fight to hold on to what we had. But I need you to let go—for me. I need to know you'll be happy again someday.

I can't stand the thought of you going through life without really smiling. Really laughing. Without being held and loved and cherished.

Tears fell in large droplets onto the paper, smudging the ink as Jennie read. There wasn't any reining them in. She swiped at the tears with the back of her hands but more just followed.

It kills me to think of someone else holding you, but this is one time I can't be selfish. I don't want you to be alone. So pick a man who makes you smile. Who makes you laugh. Who loves you and makes everything right in your world. Promise me, Bugsy. Move on.

And every once in a while, look up to the sky and let me see your gorgeous face. Your funny lopsided smile and your beautiful cinnamon eyes.

And for heaven's sake, if it took you longer than two years to open this letter, find him quickly! You've wasted enough time.

I'll love you always and forever,

Kyle

Jennie was laughing and crying when she heard the door open behind her. Chad sat quietly on the bed next to her without saying a word. He reached for a tissue and wiped her face for her, then passed her a plate of toast.

"Eat."

Without a word, she took the plate and handed the letter to Chad. He looked at it and looked back at her.

"Where'd this come from?" he asked.

"I've been carrying it around in my purse."

His eyebrows shot up. "You just opened it now?"

Jennie laughed and brushed at her tears with the back of her hand. "I'm slow. But apparently he knew that."

She nodded at the letter. Chad looked at her for a second but began to read.

"Bugsy?" he asked with a smile.

She smiled and nodded, biting into the hot toast as Chad continued to read.

"He was a smart man," he said when he finished the letter. "You should listen to him."

She laughed and they sat quietly while Jennie ate and Chad waited. When she finished, he took the plate from her hands and set it on the table next to the bed. He pulled her onto his lap and held her tight.

She wasn't crying anymore. She held onto Chad and let all the heartache and pain she'd been holding in for so long seep from her body. She'd never felt more emotionally drained.

But she also felt better than she had in a long time. She felt lighter, as if she'd finally lost a great load she'd carried for far too long.

She knew it was time to let Kyle go. And, she didn't need Kyle to tell her to fall in love with Chad. She'd fallen in love with him a long time ago. She had just needed Kyle to tell her it was okay to feel that way. To let Chad all the way in.

"I love you, Chad," Jennie said. "I think I always have."

She felt his head nuzzle her neck and he held her even tighter but didn't say anything for a long time. Just when she thought he wasn't going to say anything at all, he finally spoke.

"I've loved you forever, Jen. I always have and I always will."

"You're gonna marry me, right Chad?"

This got a bark of laughter from Chad.

"No."

"What?" Jennie sat up and put both hands on his face, pulling his head up to face her. "What do you mean?"

"You're not allowed to propose to me, Jennie. That's my job. Besides, you did it wrong. You don't have a ring or anything. You're supposed to be down on one knee with a ring when you propose."

"I'd look silly if I did that." She leaned back and looked at him. "You chauvinist pig. That's, that's... You can't do that. You're turning me down? You're not going to marry me?"

"Nope." He smiled and touched her lips with his finger, gently, then brushed his lips to hers. "I'm turning you down."

"What! You can't do that. You love me. I'm having your baby. You have to marry me!"

He grinned and shook his head.

"I'll let you help me name the baby if you marry me," she said, opening the negotiations.

Chad laughed and flipped Jennie under him, coming down on top of her. He kissed her long and hard, erasing her indignation. Erasing all thoughts from her head, ending all negotiations.

He quickly stripped her of her clothes, following with his own. He turned her on her side and lay next to her, slipping easily into her wet folds, plunging slowly but deeply into her. He drew gasp after gasp of pure pleasure from her as he took them both to climax in the gentlest lovemaking Jennie had ever felt.

And, Jennie felt whole again. The pieces of her life that had been so torn apart had been put back together. The end product didn't look the same as it once had, but that was okay.

She knew she would love this life as much as she'd loved her life with Kyle. And she knew Kyle would want it that way.

CHAPTER 36

$\mathcal{J}$ ennie watched Chad get ready for the fake meeting with Burke and Mike. After hearing about the arson attempt, Agent Burke told Chad he planned to fly up and take Jennie's statement personally.

Chad and Mike weren't sure whether that made him seem more or less guilty. It was possible he wanted to be here to make sure his witness was safe or it could mean he wanted to be here to be sure Bandon got the job done and took Jennie out.

Either way, they decided not to take any chances. Jennie would be nowhere near the meeting. She'd stay locked away in Chad's condo while they went to see Burke.

They considered moving her to a hotel, but the condo had doormen on twenty-four-seven who wouldn't let a soul up into the condo without Chad or Jennie's permission, and none of the stairwells or elevators could be accessed without an electronic keycode. It would be much harder for anyone to access than a hotel where people could come and go and blend in with ease.

Jennie felt tears burn behind her eyes as she kissed Chad good-bye.

"Hey," he said, tilting her head to force her to meet his eyes.

"I'll be right back, Jen. I promise. A couple of hours and all this will be over."

She nodded, but she was about to lose her battle with the tears. When she tried to speak the tears fell.

"I can't lose you, too, Chad. I can't go through that again," she said, panic rising in her lungs, threatening to suffocate her if she didn't get it under control. Her heart was beating so fast, she wondered if it would hurt the baby if she didn't find a way to calm down, but she couldn't.

He wrapped his arms around her and lifted her off the floor, holding her tight.

"You won't lose me," he whispered in her ear, his voice husky. "I'm not going anywhere, I promise. I'll be back here, forcing you to eat healthy meals and bugging you about having too many pastries before you know it. Hell, you'll be so tired of me, you'll probably be kicking me out of my own house by tomorrow night. I promise."

She nodded but held tight for a few more minutes, wrapped around him, memorizing the feel of him, his steady, quiet strength.

She kissed him hard and let go, letting him walk away, but praying he'd be back and this would all be over soon.

Chad pulled into the hotel parking lot. They'd fed the location to Burke the day before so Burke would have plenty of time to get the false lead to Bandon.

Only Burke's direct supervisor, AUSA Waters and those directly involved in the sting knew the location was a setup and Jennie would be hiding at Chad's house instead of showing up for the meet. The agents at the sting had been handpicked by Mike, and Chad trusted Mike not to use anyone he wasn't one hundred percent sure about.

Chad knew that Burke and Mike would already be waiting in the room the bureau had rented for the meeting. Since Burke had never met Jennie, it had been easy for Mike to find a smaller female agent with similar hair color to play the part of Jennie.

Agent Kirsten Danners sat next to Chad in the cab of his truck, a bullet-proof vest under her clothing, ready to put her life on the line to draw out a killer. Her hair was too red to be Jennie, but it would have to do. It would be close enough to fool anyone who had a general description of Jennie and happened to be watching them enter or exit the building.

Chad scanned the parking lot as they entered the building and he knew Agent Danners would do the same. His eyes flicked to rooftops, windows, and surrounding cars. No sign of anyone suspicious, but he did spot the two backup agents they had planted outside.

One agent was up on a telephone pole, his position as a fake repairman giving him a good eagle-eye view of the surrounding area. The other was dressed as a maintenance worker and pushed a cart from trash can to trash can emptying the garbage liners and picking up any litter on his route.

The arsonists Bandon had sent to Jennie's parents' house were pretty inexperienced guys. Just hired muscle following directions, but so far, they weren't spilling anything to the police. Chad was hoping Bandon would show up to do the job himself this time instead of sending anyone else who might screw it up again.

As Chad walked across the parking lot with Danners at his side, he felt the hairs on the back of his neck stand on end. Something didn't feel right about this, but he couldn't put his finger on what it was.

His eyes roamed the area once again. Nothing had changed. No signs that anything had gone wrong, but he couldn't shake the uneasy feeling.

Chad and Agent Danners knocked on the door to the hotel

room and waited for Mike to open the door. When he did, Chad stepped through first, quickly taking in the room. Only Agent Burke sat in the room. The curtains had been drawn and Burke had a notepad in front of him ready to take notes.

"You cleared the room?" Chad asked Mike, knowing the answer but needing to ask anyway.

Mike nodded and then introduced Chad and Danners to Agent Burke, introducing Danners as Jennie Evans. Chad kept a protective hand on Danners as he guided her to the sofa, as he would have if Danners were Jennie.

He watched Burke closely, assessing his body language. Burke didn't bat an eye when the agent was introduced as Jennie. He appeared to have no idea this wasn't the real Jennie.

Mike and Agent Danners sat on the sofa across from Burke but Chad stood, watching Burke.

Burke leaned forward, appearing earnest as he started his interview. He didn't bother to try to set his witness at ease before jumping right into questioning her, but he was gentle in his questioning.

"Before we go into the details of your trip to Florida, I want to talk about last night a bit, Jennie. We need to get to the bottom of who tried to set your parents' house on fire," Burke said. When he continued, he looked up at Chad and then back to the fake Jennie. "Who knew you were coming home last night?"

As Agent Danners answered him, feeding him the information she'd been given for her role as Jennie, Chad continued to watch Burke. There wasn't a single clue that he was being anything other than honest in his line of questioning.

No eye-blocking behavior like lowering of his eyelids or rubbing an eye. He didn't engage in any pacifying behaviors like tugging at his collar or rubbing the back of his neck. It didn't mean he wasn't lying, especially since he would have received training in the area of body language and deceit as an FBI agent, but Chad was pretty damn good at spotting a lie. He wasn't seeing anything but honesty as he looked at Burke.

He caught Mike's eye and he knew Mike was thinking the same thing. Burke was questioning Agent Danners as if he genuinely wanted to get to find out who was behind the attempted arson the night before.

If he'd been the one to leak the information, it was unlikely he'd raise the issue first. It was more likely he would have had an ambush out in the parking lot that Danners and Chad would have had to deal with on the way in.

Mike spoke up, breaking into the conversation Burke was having with Danners. "Agent Burke, I think we need to follow all possible avenues here. Who did you contact after hearing from Chad about Jennie's whereabouts last night?"

Burke's eyes shot to Mike first then to Chad and all Chad saw was genuine shock, followed by anger. Mike diffused his anger by holding up a hand in appeasement.

"I only ask because we need to trace all possible avenues of a leak. We need to know who you passed the info on to, so we can track those leads," Mike said.

Burke nodded and the anger seeped from him but you could still see a hint of indignation at having another agent question him. Mike outranked Burke as a Supervisory Special Agent, so Chad knew Burke wasn't likely to argue.

Mike's phone rang as Burke opened his mouth to speak. Mike glanced at the screen before taking the call with an apologetic look to the group. They listened as he grunted a couple of responses then looked up at Chad with startled eyes.

"What is it?" Chad asked as soon as Mike ended the call.

"I had one of my people running down anything we could find on the two men who tried to start the fire at Jennie's parent's house. They're out on bail on charges of grand larceny in an auto theft ring in Florida. The AUSA on their case is Caroline Waters," Mike said.

Agent Burke cursed. "I only told three people of your whereabouts. I left a voicemail for the Special Agent in Charge of the New Haven field office to see if she could send a field agent out to Torrington to take Jennie's statement. I sent an email to my supervisor. The third person was AUSA Waters. I copied her on the email. If she gets her emails on her phone like I do, she would have seen it shortly after you contacted me," Agent Burke said.

Chad didn't wait to hear any more and neither did Mike. They moved in tandem toward the door as Chad took his phone out of his pocket. "We need to get to Jennie."

As Mike drove, Chad tried to reach Jennie on her phone, but she didn't pick up. He hung up and sent a text telling her not let anyone in. As soon as that went through, he tried calling again.

He couldn't lose her now.

Not now when they'd only really just found each other.

CHAPTER 37

*J*ennie paced Chad's condo, walking from one room to the next. She'd settle for a bit in one room, pick up a book and try to read or pull out a carton of milk and a glass to pour a drink, before abandoning it and moving to another room. She couldn't seem to settle herself at all.

She knew the smart choice had been for her to stay behind, but waiting for Chad to come back to her wasn't easy. It was probably the hardest thing she'd had to do in the nightmare that had become her existence since she'd met the Masters brothers.

She knew Chad would call or text as soon as they had either Burke or Bandon or both men in custody so she stared at her cell phone relentlessly.

Realistically, she knew it wouldn't ring for at least a couple of hours, if that soon. She watched it just the same, willing it to ring. She just needed to hear his voice and know he was safe, know he was coming home to her.

Jennie startled when the landline rang in Chad's condo a half hour after he left. She knew the landline was actually only there for the doorman to call up to the condo. Though it wasn't used for anything else, she still worried that someone was calling that number to tell her something had happened.

That things had gone wrong and Chad wouldn't be coming home to her.

Fear clenched in her stomach as she crossed to the cordless phone that sat in its cradle on the kitchen counter.

"Hello?" she answered.

"Ms. Evans? It's Bernard from downstairs." She let out a breath as she recognized the doorman. "There's a Caroline Waters here to see you. Says she's with the United States Attorney's office. She has credentials and she said Mr. Thompson sent her to sit with you. She said you would understand why. Do you want me to send her up, Ms. Evans?"

"Oh." Chad hadn't told her he would be sending anyone, but it made sense that the attorney for the case would want to speak with her. "Are you sure she has identification?"

"Yes, ma'am, but I can tell her to wait until Mr. Thompson returns, if you'd like."

"No, no. That's all right. Send her up please."

"Yes, ma'am."

The phone went dead and Jennie put it down on the counter and went to open the door to the condo. The ping of the elevator door came a minute later and a sharply dressed woman a few years older than Jennie came down the hall.

"Hi," Jennie greeted her as she came to a stop outside the door.

"Hello Ms. Evans. I'm Caroline Waters." The woman glanced around the hallway as she spoke and Jennie thought she looked nervous. Maybe something had happened with the meeting and Chad had sent this woman because Jennie was in danger.

"Come inside. We can talk in here. Is everything going okay at the meeting?" Jennie asked as she opened the door to Ms. Waters.

"Oh, yes. Just fine, I'm sure," Ms. Waters said. "I'm only here to take your statement. I'll get the details from you and then my office will write everything up in an affidavit for you to sign later."

Jennie nodded, leading Ms. Waters to the couch in the living room. When they were settled on the couch, the attorney took a notepad out of her bag and began to scribble notes as they talked.

"So, Ms. Evans, I understand you went to the Masters' resort to investigate the resort for a potential purchaser, is that right?"

Jennie nodded. "Yes, that's right."

"Tell me what you witnessed at the Masters' resort during your trip to Florida," Ms. Waters said, looking at Jennie expectantly.

Even so, something in the woman's eyes was cold and dead. Jennie didn't know if she was being foolish or if she should listen to whatever it was that was telling her this woman wasn't here for the right reasons.

Jennie shook off her hesitation. The lawyers at Sutton Capital had gone over her statement with her and told her what to expect. This conversation didn't seem all that far off the mark. Jennie described what she'd overheard in the hallway outside the Masters brothers' office, staying with a factual description rather than any narrative or opinions, as the Sutton lawyers had told her to do.

"I see. And was anyone else with you at this time?"

The tone of Ms. Water's voice was calm, but Jennie could tell it was forced. There was now something very 'off' about the attorney's whole demeanor. It looked like the lawyer was feeling more anxious than Jennie felt, which didn't seem right at all.

Why would the lawyer on the case be so nervous? There was nothing Jennie could pinpoint to tell her for sure that something was wrong, but she felt it just the same.

Jennie heard her cell phone ring and rose to pick it up, but Ms. Waters' hand shot out, gripping Jennie's arm.

Jennie whipped around to look at the woman and Ms. Waters released her hand as if she realized how much she'd overreacted. But, the damage was done. Jennie was sure something was wrong.

"I'd really like to finish this quickly, Jennie. If you could talk me through this I'll be out of your hair in no time," Ms. Waters said. "I need to be sure no one else was with you when you heard these statements. I mean, was there anyone else with you that I need to be speaking with?"

Cold shivers ran up Jennie's spine and she felt the urgent need to get away from the woman who was staring intently at her. Every cell in Jennie's body seemed to be screaming at her, telling her to get away.

Her hand dropped to her stomach, as if she could somehow cover the baby to protect it from whatever was about to happen.

Jennie's phone beeped, indicating an incoming text message and almost immediately began to ring again. She stood up, not knowing what she should do, but knowing she needed to put some distance between her and this woman.

"I'm going to get that—"

In that moment, several things seemed to happen at once. Chad and Mike burst through the door at the same time Jennie saw Caroline Waters shoot to her feet, pulling a gun out of her purse.

Jennie's blood ran cold. Somehow in that moment, she wasn't frightened for herself; she was terrified for Chad. If she lost him, she knew she wouldn't live through it.

She wasn't strong enough to go through that again. Not this time.

She was vaguely aware of Mike talking to Caroline. Caroline's arm shook as she tried to hold the gun on all three of them. Chad was talking to Jennie, reaching for her, telling her to come to him.

She stood several feet from Caroline and across the room from Chad. Jennie knew Chad wanted her near him so he could protect her. He had turned from the Chad she knew into a highly trained warrior, ready to fight for her, ready to die for her.

But, Jennie couldn't let that happen.

The world seemed to slow down in that moment. The tension was almost palpable and Jennie knew this would end badly. She could feel it in the cold dread crawling up her spine. She looked from Chad to Caroline and back again.

Chad was still talking but Jennie couldn't hear what he was saying. She knew Caroline would start shooting her way out of the room if the desperate, cornered look on her face was any indication.

"No," Jennie whispered. She wasn't speaking to Caroline or Chad or even herself, for that matter.

She was speaking to the universe in general. To whatever it was that thought it was okay to take two men from her. To take first her husband and now the father of her unborn child. Jennie's fists clenched and she felt the bite of her nails breaking the skin of her palms.

"No."

She wouldn't let this happen. She lost Kyle, but there was no way Jennie would lose Chad, too. She lunged at Caroline, aware in the back of her mind that Chad was screaming at her and charging for her. Jennie heard a gunshot but didn't feel anything as she tackled Caroline to the ground.

The gunshot was louder than she expected it to be. Her ears were ringing and she thought to herself that the whole world seemed to be moving in slow motion. Everything sounded fuzzy. Everything looked fuzzy, she thought with a strange dazed feeling.

Jennie felt Chad's arms around her, lifting her as she saw Mike subdue Caroline. He secured the gun Caroline had dropped when she fell to the ground.

Jennie turned to Chad and ran her hands over him, frantically trying to figure out where he'd been shot. As she ran her hands over his chest, his arms, desperate to know where he'd been hit, he lifted her up.

He ran through the door with her, holding her in his arms. Jennie saw other agents in the hallway and heard someone call out that an ambulance was waiting downstairs.

Why is Chad carrying me if he needs an ambulance? This is so silly.

She looked into his face as he entered the elevator and pushed the button. He cradled her in his arms and was talking to her, but she couldn't hear him over the ringing in her ears. Jennie must have been closer than she realized to Caroline's gun when it went off.

She followed Chad's line of sight to her arm and stared in shock at the blood pouring down her arm and dripping onto her hand. Chad's hand was wrapped around her forearm, applying pressure to try to slow the bleeding, but the blood was seeping through his fingers. It was only after seeing it that her body seemed to register the sensations, the pain.

The blood was hotter than she'd thought it would be as it dripped over her hand and onto the elevator floor. And her arm felt numb, except for the back of it.

The back of her arm felt like someone had dug into it with a stick made out of salt. It burned like nothing she'd ever felt before. The pain was so intense, her breath seemed to stop and she stared up at Chad, finally understanding.

He hadn't been shot.

She had.

CHAPTER 38

C had tried to calm himself as he waited for the elevator to make the interminably long ride to the lobby of his building. He knew the truth about gunshot wounds. It was a myth from the movies and television that you could get shot with a through and through in the arm and not have any real damage.

In reality, the arm was full of arteries and nerves. Jennie could bleed out or lose enough blood to harm the baby in a matter of minutes if the bullet hit the right spot. She could permanently lose some of the use of her arm or the feeling in her hand. If the bone was shattered, fragments of that bone could hit other arteries and nerves, multiplying the damage.

Flashes of Chad's fallen team members, their eyes vacant and unseeing, tore at him as he tried to stay focused on Jennie.

When he'd seen her dive for Caroline, throwing herself between Chad and the gun, he nearly lost it. The fact he had survived two tours of duty in war zones and years of dangerous privately funded missions, would mean nothing if he couldn't share his life with Jennie.

He knew then that he needed Jennie in his life more than he'd ever needed anyone.

He saw the moment she realized she'd been shot. He watched

as the pain kicked in and he thought to himself as he stepped off the elevator with her in his arms, that he'd give anything to have taken that bullet for her. He'd trade her pain and take it on as his own in a heartbeat if he could.

He was met in the lobby by two EMTs with a gurney and he knew one of the agents must have called down to the ambulance. He placed her on the gurney and told them she was pregnant. He took her good hand in his as he raced alongside to the ambulance where a pressure bandage was applied over her wound.

"She's pregnant. Thirteen weeks along," he said.

Jennie was getting pale and Chad knew she was losing blood fast.

He followed the gurney into the ambulance, staying out of the way as he watched the EMT hang a clear bag above her and sink a needle into her good hand.

He knew it would most likely be saline. He'd seen it used in helicopter evacs in the military. Since they couldn't carry around blood on an ambulance, they'd try to compensate for the blood loss with saline until they got her to the hospital.

He kept his eyes on her face during what seemed like the longest ride of his life. His only thoughts were of Jennie and the baby. If he lost them now, he didn't know what he'd do.

CHAPTER 39

*C*had was sitting, hunched over, head in his hands in the hospital waiting room an hour later when the room began to fill. Jennie and Kyle's parents arrived first, followed closely by Chad's mom.

Chad had never been so happy to see his mother in his life. He felt like he was ten years old again as she wrapped her arms around him and held him while he told her about Jennie and the baby.

Kelly, Jack, Andrew, and Jill arrived next with Mrs. Poole and Roark Walker in tow. She had packed a large thermos with hot chocolate and a plate of homemade cookies for Chad, but he couldn't even think about eating until he knew what was going on with Jennie.

Kelly sat on one side of him, her fingers laced in his, clinging tightly to him while his mother sat on the other side of him murmuring to him over and over that Jennie and the baby would be all right.

Roark sat across from Chad. He was the head of the legal department at Sutton but he was also a longtime family friend. He leaned over and put a warm hand on Chad's forearm and squeezed.

Roark had lost his wife years before. He didn't say anything to Chad. Probably knew better than anyone that there was nothing he could say at this point to make things better. But he was there for Chad, just as all of them were.

Mrs. Poole put the plate of cookies in Roark's hands and leaned in to hug Chad. She was soft and warm and he let himself lean into her for a minute.

When he pulled back, she patted his cheek and then went to sit with Jack and Kelly across from him. Jack gave Chad a nod and Chad knew Jack would do anything he could to help. All Chad would have to do is ask.

But there wasn't a damned thing any of them could do but wait, and that was killing him.

He looked up to see Jennie's obstetrician walked into the waiting room and scanned for him. He hadn't met her but he'd seen her picture online when he had researched for the best doctor money could buy in New Haven.

"Dr. Kash?" he said as he stood and approached her.

"Are you Chad?" she asked and he liked her right away. She had a no-nonsense tone to her and even though she stood about five feet tall to his nearly six and a half feet, she didn't shrink from him at all when he approached.

"Yeah, that's me. Any news on Jennie and the baby?"

He could practically feel the whole room holding its collective breath behind him and he knew he wouldn't be able to breathe right until he knew she and the baby were okay.

It suddenly struck him that if she lost the baby, he would have to tell her and that would crush her. He said another prayer for his child and the woman he loved as he waited for the doctor to give him an update.

"They've got her in surgery right now, but it looks like she was very lucky. She lost a lot of blood, but the EMTs got her here quickly and we took her straight into surgery. Right now, the baby looks good. I came out to tell you they're monitoring the fetal heart rate and looking for any signs of stress while they work on Jennie. I'll go back in there with her until they finish up.

"The bullet nicked her brachial artery but missed the bone, so she should regain the use of her arm after some physical therapy. I'll have the surgeon come out and update you after they repair the artery. They'll have to monitor the repair for a bit while she's still on the table to be sure it holds and to be sure blood is flowing well through the artery after the stitches are in place," the doctor explained.

Chad nodded, feeling somewhat numb, but at least now he had some idea of what was going on. He felt his mom's hands on his arm again and let her lead him back to the chairs, where he sat and began to breathe again. A world without Jennie would have been too difficult to bear.

Jennie opened her eyes and tried to swallow, but her throat was dry and scratchy. Chad was right there, putting a straw to her lips and whispering to her to drink.

She took a sip of the cold liquid and licked her lips, before testing her voice. The room was unfamiliar, but it quickly registered that she was in a hospital room.

"What happened?"

"Well, Jennie," Chad said, and she could see the small tick in his jaw that meant he was clenching it and grinding his teeth. "Let's review what happened, shall we?"

She was startled to hear the tone in his voice but she could see the love in his eyes.

She opened her mouth to speak but Chad continued before she could argue.

"When faced with a desperate, panicked woman holding a deadly weapon, you apparently looked at the situation, and in all your infinite wisdom chose to tackle her. You, the pregnant woman with no training in disarming crazed gun-toting people, thought you could handle the situation better than a trained FBI agent and a former Army Ranger with years' worth of bad-guy-tackling experience."

"The baby! Oh, God, Chad, please. Is the baby—"

"The baby's okay," he said, his voice as soft as his eyes now. "Dr. Kash has been by to check several times. No problems." He pushed Jennie's hair back from her face as he spoke and she breathed easier, knowing Dr. Kash had checked the baby.

"Bad-guy-tackling experience, huh?" Jennie asked.

"What the hell were you thinking, Jen?" Chad's voice cracked as he spoke and she knew he was fighting to stay calm.

"That I love you," she said.

"If you loved me you wouldn't keep taking years off my life. I swear, Jennie, if you ever jump in front of a gun for me again, I'll strangle you myself."

He softened the effect of his words a bit when he took her hand in his and kissed the palm of it more gently than anyone his size should be able to.

He brought the straw to her lips again to let her take another sip of water. A nurse came in and began to buzz around them, checking the machines and bags of fluids that surrounded Jennie.

"Does this mean you're going to marry me, Chad?" Jennie asked.

"No. I'm still not marrying you."

Jennie almost laughed when she saw the nurse's frown as the woman left the room.

"What! Chad you can't do that. This is crazy. I'm having your baby. I took a bullet for you. I saved your life. You have to marry me now."

He just laughed at her as he laced his fingers through hers, then brought her hand to his lips once again. Jennie's mother poked her head through the door of the room, letting Chad off the hook.

"The nurse said you were awake, sweetheart," she said and Jennie could tell she was trying to stay calm but the tears were evident in her eyes and her voice.

"Hi, Mom," Jennie said and the tears began to flow as her mother came and held her other hand.

Her father stepped into the room next. "Chad, Mike's out here to see you."

Chad and Mr. Davies switched places as Chad went to see Mike. Jennie let her parents wrap their arms around her and hold her despite the wires and tubes that still pumped liquids into her and monitored her baby.

She needed to be held right now. She needed to know everything was okay. That they had survived this and come out on the other side. That everything was okay now.

CHAPTER 40

"*H*ey, Mike. You look like shit," Chad said as he met his friend down the hall from Jennie's room. "Get anything out of Waters?"

The two men shook hands, but Mike pulled Chad in to hug him and Chad didn't try to fight it. It felt good to be surrounded by his friends and family right now.

"How's Jennie?"

"Good. She and the baby are doing okay. Jennie has to stay here for a few more days but the bullet didn't hit the bone."

Mike nodded. They'd both seen enough injuries to know this could have been a lot worse.

"We found Rick Bandon trying to board a flight for France," Mike said. "As soon as we brought him in, he and Caroline Waters began spouting information faster than we could record it all, each trying to make the best deal. I think Bandon might win because he has records of at least ten other Florida officials that were taking bribes and having him clean money for them.

"He wasn't just running things through Florifish. He had four other businesses set up with the other officials so he could distribute the clean money to them without it showing up in someone's account as not legitimate. Waters is willing to testify that Bandon killed the Masters brothers, though, so she's got that going for her," Mike said as the two men walked down the hall toward a row of vending machines.

Chad grimaced at the choice of 'meals' in the machine. A candy bar or a bag of chips.

"Not that I'm complaining because I think this could have been a lot worse than it was, but why didn't Bandon come after Jennie himself?" Chad asked.

"Caroline Waters claimed she talked him into letting her go in first to see if Jennie knew anything that could implicate either of them. After what he did to the Masters brothers, she said she stepped in to try to protect Jennie, then panicked when you and I came in the door. I don't know if she's telling the truth, but it makes sense. If Bandon was nearby and saw the ambulance and marked cars outside your building, it would have sent him running to the airport. France won't extradite to the US if the death penalty is on the table, so he must have thought he'd be pretty safe there."

"Chad!" Jack's voice rang out down the hall and Chad looked up to see his cousin coming toward him, followed by Andrew and Jill.

"Hey, guys," Chad said, turning to his friends. "Jennie's awake. Her parents are in with her now."

"I'm gonna get going, Chad. I'll keep you posted. I'm glad to hear Jennie and the baby are okay," Mike said as he slapped Chad on the back and walked down the hall.

Chad wasn't sure how he'd repay Mike for all he'd done to help them through this, but some day he'd find a way.

"We brought you food," Jill said, holding out a takeout bag. He grabbed her in a bear hug when he smelled Mexican food coming from the bag. He hadn't eaten in hours but he wasn't about to leave the hospital any time soon. The nurses had all tried to get him to go home and rest but he'd looked at them like they'd suggested he cut off his own head. He didn't know why anyone would think he'd leave Jennie. As long as she was in the hospital, that's where he'd be.

"You're the best, Jill," Chad said as he released Andrew's wife.

"Hey, we helped get that food. Don't we get any credit?" Andrew asked gesturing to him and Jack.

"You guys are still in the dog house for starting this whole mess. I'll set Jennie on you when she gets out of here and you can beg her forgiveness for getting her into all this with your scheming and lies."

Andrew and Jack shifted on their feet, looking sufficiently chagrined. Chad figured he'd draw this out a bit longer before letting them off the hook, but Jennie's parents came out, interrupting Chad's fun.

"Where are Kelly and Maddy?" Chad asked.

"They went back to the house with Mrs. Poole. Maddy needed to nap and Mrs. Poole wants to start cooking. I think her plan is to fill your freezer with enough food to last you and Jennie the next year or so," Jack said with a grin.

Mrs. Poole was officially Jack and Kelly's housekeeper, but she acted as mother hen to all of them. Chad knew Jack wasn't exaggerating about the amount of food headed for his freezer.

They all talked for a few more minutes and then hugged Chad good-bye so he could go back to sit with Jennie.

She'd fallen asleep so he ate the take-out food quietly and then turned out the light. He knew the nurses would be in to check her and the fetal monitor the doctor wanted Jennie hooked up to for a while longer. They both needed to sleep while they could.

Chad lay his head down on the edge of Jennie's bed and put one arm over her legs. He'd slept in a lot worse places than this and he wasn't leaving Jennie's side until it was time to take her home.

CHAPTER 41

ennie was released from the hospital four days later. They didn't go back to Chad's condo. He had a cleaning company come in and clean up the crime scene and he told Jennie he planned to put it on the market.

They'd stay in her house for now, where she was comfortable and Zeke had a backyard. She insisted Chad could only stay until his condo had been cleaned unless he planned on marrying her.

Of course, this news was delivered with her good fist on her hip and as much fire as she could muster with a bullet wound keeping her mildy subdued.

Jennie had seen all of her friends in the hospital but only in groups of two for short visits at a time and she was anxious to see them all again.

A week after leaving the hospital, they headed into the offices of Sutton Capital, but it wasn't for work.

Jennie's arm was in a sling and she was still taking pain medicine on a round-the-clock schedule. Not to mention moving a little stiffly.

Chad, of course, wouldn't leave her side. And there had been more than a few never-take-a-bullet-for-me-again speeches in the last week.

Jennie couldn't regret anything she'd done, though. She loved Chad with everything she was. It wasn't more or less than she'd loved Kyle. It was different. Different but no less whole and deep and profound. And she was grateful for having found the love of two men in her lifetime.

The elevator doors slid open on the twenty-sixth floor revealing a large banner hanging in the Sutton lobby that read "Kill it, Sam!"

The right side of the banner boasted the logo for Sam's game, Tangled Legacy, with the dragon wings and a fairy dagger that one of Sam's friends had drawn for her. The man was a talented graphic designer and the logo looked slick.

Jennie grinned. "Congratulations would have been too boring."

Chad kept a hand on her back as they wove through the crowd, saying hello and hugging coworkers and friends. When they got to the main floor of the office, they found many of their coworkers planted in front of computers, all waiting for the release of Samantha's game.

Others were out on the rooftop patio where a fire crackled in the firepit and Sam stood with Jill and Andrew.

They were watching a tablet Andrew held, but Samantha had covered her face with her hands.

"I can't watch. What if there are glitches?"

Andrew laughed. "I doubt that."

Jill put an arm around Sam. "You've checked everything several thousand times. There won't be any glitches."

Jill looked up and saw Chad and Jennie, waving with her hand. "Come on, it's almost time."

Samantha leaned in to hug Jennie, careful of her arm.

"I'm so proud of you, Sam," Chad said, taking his turn for a hug.

Samantha bit her lip and tugged at her long black hair, nerves getting the better of her. It was a good thing Jack had been able to convince Samantha to hire a company to handle the release of the game. That way, Sam could be as nervous and anxious as she wanted and not let those nerves affect hitting the go button when the time was right.

Jennie looked up to see Jack leading Kelly through the crowd toward them, but since everyone they passed stopped them to look down into the car seat he was carrying, Jennie knew it would take a while for them to make it to them.

Still, they waited and when the couple made it to them, there was another round of hugs all around.

Jennie looked down into the car seat at Maddy, who somehow slept through all the noise around her. Tiny bubbles of spit formed one her little pink lips as she breathed and Jennie put her hand down to her stomach, still not able to really believe she would have her own baby in a matter of months.

She looked up at Chad, who was hugging Jack and smiled. He was going to be such a good dad. Neither one of them had a clue what they were doing in the parenting department, but she knew he would be a steady rock to her in the coming years of turmoil and chaos.

Inside, the people in front of computers started a countdown chant, letting them all know the time for the game to go live was coming near.

"Ten...nine...eight..."

"Oh God," Sam said.

Jennie wrapped her good arm around Samantha while Chad wrapped his arm around her from the other side.

They all joined the count. "Seven...six...five...four..."

Samantha closed her eyes.

"Three...two...one!"

There was silence as the group waited.

Inside, a cheer went up from the people waiting for the game to go live.

And then there were shouts as the game started and they

called out about the sick graphics and the avatars they were all choosing. There was something called the Vessel they all needed to find in the first quest, but Jennie knew from playing the game herself during the beta stage that they'd have to bond with a dragon first before they could hunt down the vessel.

Bonding with a dragon meant killing whatever threatened the dragon first, and that often meant battling the twisted fairies and noir gnomes.

Jennie watched Samantha's face as they continued to listen to their coworkers playing the game in the other room.

"Sam, this is epic!"

"Did you see that?"

"My dragon is so beautiful!"

She saw the moment Sam started to realize what was happening.

Kelly grinned and pushed the tablet toward Sam. "Look at those numbers, Samantha."

They were watching the people signing onto the game in real time and the number was climbing fast. Ten thousand, twelve, fifteen, twenty-five thousand.

Chad hugged Samantha. "You did it, Sam. They love it."

It was a good feeling seeing their friend succeed at something she'd been working so hard at for such a long time. Sam and computers was a natural thing but Jennie knew Samantha had been worried about the more creative aspects of building the world for her game.

Coming up with the magical rules and quests the players would go on wasn't easy. So far, there were seventeen levels to the game and Sam was working on adding more.

Jennie hugged Samantha tight and let herself revel in the feel of all the good things she'd found in this world. She had Chad and his love, but she also had good friends she loved. She had a job she was looking forward to getting back to soon. She had her family.

She blinked back tears as she thought about all the blessings in her world. Yes, she'd lived through tragedy and heartache, but she was on the other side of it now, and she couldn't be more grateful.

Chad squeezed her hand and leaned down to whisper in her ear.

"You alright, Jen?"

She looked up and squeezed his hand back. "Better than alright."

He dropped a kiss to her lips, one she wished he'd take deeper. He pulled back and smiled and his look told her he knew exactly what she was thinking.

He leaned in and brushed his lips over hers again, this time only giving her a hint of contact before pulling back.

She growled at him and he laughed. He knew exactly what he was doing to her and he was having entirely too much fun with that knowledge.

She narrowed her eyes. Payback was going to be fun.

CHAPTER 42

*T*hanks to Mrs. Poole, Kelly and Jack were back to hosting get-togethers at their house a month later. Jennie and Chad were heading down to Jack and Kelly's house for an official welcome-home-Jennie party. She had laughed when Kelly suggested it since she'd been home over a month.

Kelly would use any excuse to host a party. Mrs. Poole alternated between shooing Roark away from her and putting him to work spreading pies and cookies out on a table.

Kelly had invited Jennie's family and Kyle's parents had driven down for the event. It amazed Jennie to see them embrace Chad and to see the way Chad responded to them.

He seemed to treat Kyle's parents as if they were simply an extra set of parents to Jennie. It made her feel secure for some reason, knowing she could keep that part of her life intact instead of losing them as she moved on to find new love with Chad.

She sat, surrounded by friends and family, smiling and laughing, her heart free and light for the first time in a very long time. She felt like she'd come through a long hard winter and was seeing the sun for the first time.

Everyone wanted a play-by-play of the whole story, from the trip to Florida to the shooting, even though by now, everyone had heard it before. She sat back and let Chad and her parents tell the tale.

It was surreal listening to them tell her story. Chad skimmed quickly over her heartache over Kyle's death. She assumed that was to spare her from reliving it, but she felt oddly at ease. She would always love Kyle, but the pain didn't cut as deeply anymore.

Most likely, her pain at losing Kyle had lingered for so long and had been so great because she had felt she had a hand in his death. When her parents and Kyle's parents convinced her she didn't, it was as if they set her free. Set her heart free too.

"I've asked him to marry me six times in the last month, but he said no," Jennie piped up as Chad finished the story.

Chad's mother smacked him on the back of his shoulder from her position at his side. Jennie guessed she would have liked to target the back of his head, but Mabry couldn't reach that high on Chad when he was standing up.

"Oh, you'll marry her, all right, mister," Mabry said.

Chad only laughed and before Jennie could process what was going on, he was down on one knee in front of her. He pulled a ring from his pocket.

"When did you get a ring? We've been running from killers and I've been lying in the hospital with a bullet meant for you in my arm and you've been driving me to physical therapy for a month...and y-you went ring shopping somewhere in all of that?" she sputtered.

He laughed. "They took the bullet out Jennie. You didn't lie around with a bullet in your arm. And, I've had this ring for months. Before we went on the run." He smiled and then he took her left hand in his.

As he spoke, he slipped the ring on Jennie's finger. "Will you marry me, Jennie Evans?"

She grinned at him. "No."

She shook her head but she didn't stop him from putting the

ring on her finger and the wide smile on her face told him a different story. Apparently, everyone around her saw the same thing Chad did. He stood and lifted her in his arms, spinning her around as their friends cheered.

Jennie laughed. "I thought I told you, no."

"I heard, yes. Didn't you guys hear, yes?" Chad asked over his shoulder.

Her traitorous friends all took his side, but she only laughed. She felt lighter and happier than she'd felt in a long time.

She wrapped her arms around Chad and pulled him close. "We can negotiate this later, sweetheart," she whispered.

By now the group around them was chatting and laughing so no one heard Chad whisper back. "We can negotiate your surrender later."

She threw her head back and laughed. "I won't ever surrender."

"Oh, you'll surrender," said Chad as he captured her mouth in a heated kiss that had Jennie wondering if maybe, just maybe, she would surrender.

EPILOGUE

Chad had watched Jennie as she slept—their tiny precious daughter bundled in his arms. He was afraid to move for fear of crushing her. Twenty-two hours of labor had worn Jennie out and seeing her in so much pain had been more than he could handle.

When she'd asked for an epidural, Chad wanted to drop to his knees in thanks, knowing she'd finally get some relief. He didn't do well with seeing the woman he loved hurting.

The scar on Jennie's arm was a constant reminder of the pain he'd put her through, but it also reminded him to be so grateful for having the woman he loved in his life.

He looked down at the sweet face of his sleeping daughter and laughed when he remembered Jennie telling their friends what they'd named their child.

Princess Tiffany Tabitha Tobias Thompson. She said it with a completely straight face and sold them all on her sincerity. They'd stood there with the funniest expressions trying to find some polite response. Chad felt so sorry for them, he'd told them the baby's real name.

Ella Kylee Thompson, named after Chad's grandmother and Kyle. She was a big baby, weighing in at eight and a half pounds and measuring twenty-three inches, but she still felt so small in Chad's arms. He worried he would break her. Her foot was the size of his pinkie, but boy did she scream when she came out.

Apparently, she was not thrilled to be taken out of the warm cocoon her mother had kept her in all these months. She turned her little face purple and red and opened that mouth and let the world know she was ticked off.

And, he'd never heard anything so magical in his life.

"Hey, you." Jennie spoke quietly from the bed.

Chad smiled at her and brought Ella over, knowing she would want to nurse. The baby seemed to want to eat every few hours.

"How do you feel? Do you need anything?"

Jennie shook her head at him and looked down at Ella who now nursed hungrily. Her little eyes were already closed as though she only planned to eat and then drop right off to sleep again.

"I'm okay," Jennie said. "I want to get home to our own bed and get settled in with you and Ella."

Chad kissed her forehead and brushed the hair back from her eyes. "Soon, Jen. I'm pretty sure you have to stay here at least one day, if not two," he said with a laugh.

"Can't you bribe a doctor? Get them to let me go home?" she asked as Chad laughed at her and shook his head.

"Call some of your army buddies and have them sneak us out? It'll be a black op. They'll love it," she begged.

"I love you, Jennie Thompson," he whispered, ignoring her plotting.

"I love you, too, Boss Man," she whispered back.

Chad knew a lifetime with her wouldn't be enough, but it was a start.

And, he'd take it.

The End

. . .

Loving the Sutton Billionaires? The next book is *The Billionaire's Rock Star*. Remember Gabe Sawyer? You met him back in *Reuniting with the Billionaire* when Andrew was crazy jealous of the attention Gabe was giving Jill? It's Gabe's turn to get his happily ever after. But don't worry, I didn't make it easy in him. ;)

Grab the book here: loriryanromance.com/book/the-billionaire-rocks

STALKER NOTES (OTHERWISE KNOWN AS AUTHOR NOTES)

Thank you so much for reading Chad and Jennie's story! If you've been reading the Sutton Billionaire's story from the start, you know Chad has been there from the beginning.

What you probably don't know is that when I first created his character, I thought he was going to be a total jerk. Not a bad guy, exactly, but just someone who wasn't very nice to the people around him and who was only out for himself.

Not exactly how he turned out, huh? I kind of love it when a character or a story takes on a life of their own. I ended up having to go back and rewrite him when it became clear he just wasn't going to put up with being written the way I wanted to write him.

I'm glad it ended up that way! I bet Jennie's happy, too. He ended up being just the guy she needed in her world.

Thank you for reading them and for all the love and support you've shown me throughout my years as an author! My readers are what keep me going and let me live this amazing, extraordinary life of creativity and drama!

The next book in the series, *The Billionaire's Rock Star*, is available here.

ABOUT THE AUTHOR

Lori Ryan is a NY Times and USA Today bestselling author who writes contemporary romance and romantic suspense. She lives with an extremely understanding husband, three wonderful children, and two dogs (who are lucky they're adorable and cute because they rarely behave) in Austin, Texas. It's a bit of a zoo, but she wouldn't change a thing.

Lori published her first novel in April of 2013 and has loved every bit of the crazy adventure this career has taken her on since then. Lori loves to connect with her readers. Follow her on Facebook or Twitter or subscribe to her blog. Oh, and if you've read Lori's books and loved them, please consider leaving a review with the retailer of your choice to help other readers find her work as well! It's a tremendous honor to have her work recommended to others or written up in reviews. Lori promises to do a happy dance around her office every time you write one!

facebook.com/loriryanromance

twitter.com/Loriryanauthor

instagram.com/loriryanauthor

.

Made in the USA
Las Vegas, NV
02 March 2021